多雷插图本世界名著

老舟子行

[英]塞缪尔·泰勒·柯勒律治 著
[法]古斯塔夫·多雷 绘
朱湘 译　　武学 编

版权所有　侵权必究

图书在版编目（CIP）数据

老舟子行 / （英）塞缪尔·泰勒·柯勒律治著；（法）古斯塔夫·多雷绘；朱湘译；武学编. -- 长春：吉林出版集团股份有限公司，2025.5. --（多雷插图本世界名著）. -- ISBN 978-7-5731-6534-3

Ⅰ. I561.24

中国国家版本馆CIP数据核字第2025V5Q530号

DUOLEI CHATU BEN SHIJIE MINGZHU LAO ZHOUZI XING

多雷插图本世界名著·老舟子行

著　　者：[英]塞缪尔·泰勒·柯勒律治
绘　　者：[法]古斯塔夫·多雷
译　　者：朱　湘
编　　者：武　学
出版策划：崔文辉
项目策划：赵晓星
项目执行：于媛媛
责任编辑：姜婷婷
封面设计：观止堂_未　氓
排　　版：昌信图文

出　　版：吉林出版集团股份有限公司
　　　　　（长春市福祉大路5788号，邮政编码：130118）
发　　行：吉林出版集团译文图书经营有限公司
　　　　　（http://shop34896900.taobao.com）
电　　话：总编办 0431-81629909　营销部 0431-81629880/81629881
印　　刷：大厂回族自治县益利印刷有限公司

开　　本：787mm×1092mm　1/16
印　　张：12
字　　数：85千字
版　　次：2025年5月第1版
印　　次：2025年5月第1次印刷
书　　号：ISBN 978-7-5731-6534-3
定　　价：48.00元

印装错误请与承印厂联系　联系电话：13521219071

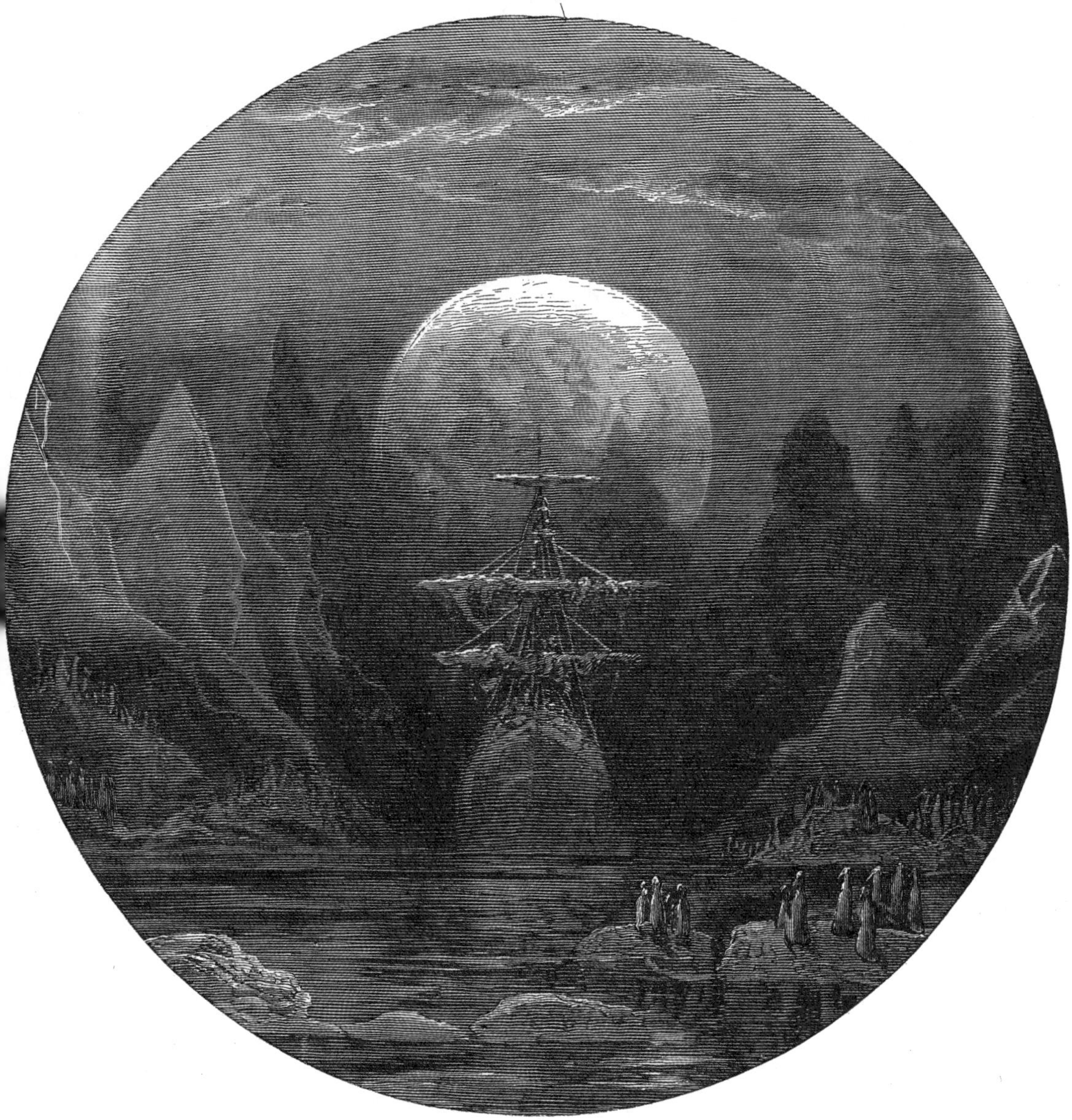

编 者 序

诗歌最好的译本，定然是出自诗人之手。因为诗人更具有对语言的敏感和对韵律的领悟，这样的直觉会使其字里行间都带有地道的"诗味儿"。诗人译诗不同于学者译诗：后者可能更合学理、更富考据；而前者则会更具诗情、更富文采。倘若诗人译者的风格与原作者的风格暗合，倘若诗人译者的外文造诣不至于造成翻译硬伤，此种译作当是天造地设的一流译作。这样的例证，古今中外俯拾皆是；单是举出中国现当代诗坛如郭沫若所译《浮士德》《鲁拜集》，穆旦所译《唐璜》《欧根·奥涅金》，以及孙大雨、卞之琳、余光中、北岛等诗人的经典译作，即可略见一斑。这便是我们在柯勒律治名诗《老舟子行》的诸多译本之中，复推出朱湘译本的原因所在。

柯勒律治是英国诗歌史上罕见以少量作品而名垂千古的诗才。较之同辈诗人连篇累牍的作品，他素为人称道的诗作，主要便是未完成的《忽必烈汗》与这部《老舟子行》。史载，这个贫病交加的卓越诗人，其创作简直就是耗费生命的工作；而他因治病，药物作用亦给他的作品带来梦幻般的奇特意境。因此，他的诗作兼具才情与激情之美；这样的作品，最适宜的当然是由诗人的生花之笔来转述，避免学者译文泥古不化、隔靴搔痒之憾。幸而我们有诗人朱湘，这位英年早逝的杰出诗人，其诗心与诗格都无愧为柯勒律治的东方继承者。朱湘以参与《诗刊》跻身新月派，其诗作秀丽娴雅，极富浪漫气息。诗史上多将其称为"东方济慈"；而他的特立独行、命途多舛，与柯勒律治则颇为神似。其所翻译的《老舟子行》，颇具中国古典诗歌的音律之美，又着力再现原作的韵律节奏，绘形绘色，堪称佳译。

  我们此次出版《老舟子行》一诗，除收录柯勒律治诗作原文和朱湘的译文之外，复收入多雷为本诗所绘全部插图，使诗坛不朽之作愈益增光。

  此外，我们保留了朱湘译本中当时文字的用法，加以校译。柯勒律治又于1817年出版此诗定本时添加若干旁注，为朱湘译本所无。考虑到这些旁注颇便读者领悟原诗，为便阅读，我们亦将其一并译出附后，以臻完璧。

目　录

　　《老舟子行》全诗分为七个部分，每一部分围绕关键事件展开。一艘经过赤道的大船如何受暴风雨驱使，闯入冰封海域？她又如何从南极北行，回到热带纬度，闯入太平洋？经历种种奇异，老舟子以何种方式重返故乡？

第一部分 / 001

第二部分 / 029

第三部分 / 047

第四部分 / 069

第五部分 / 089

第六部分 / 119

第七部分 / 149

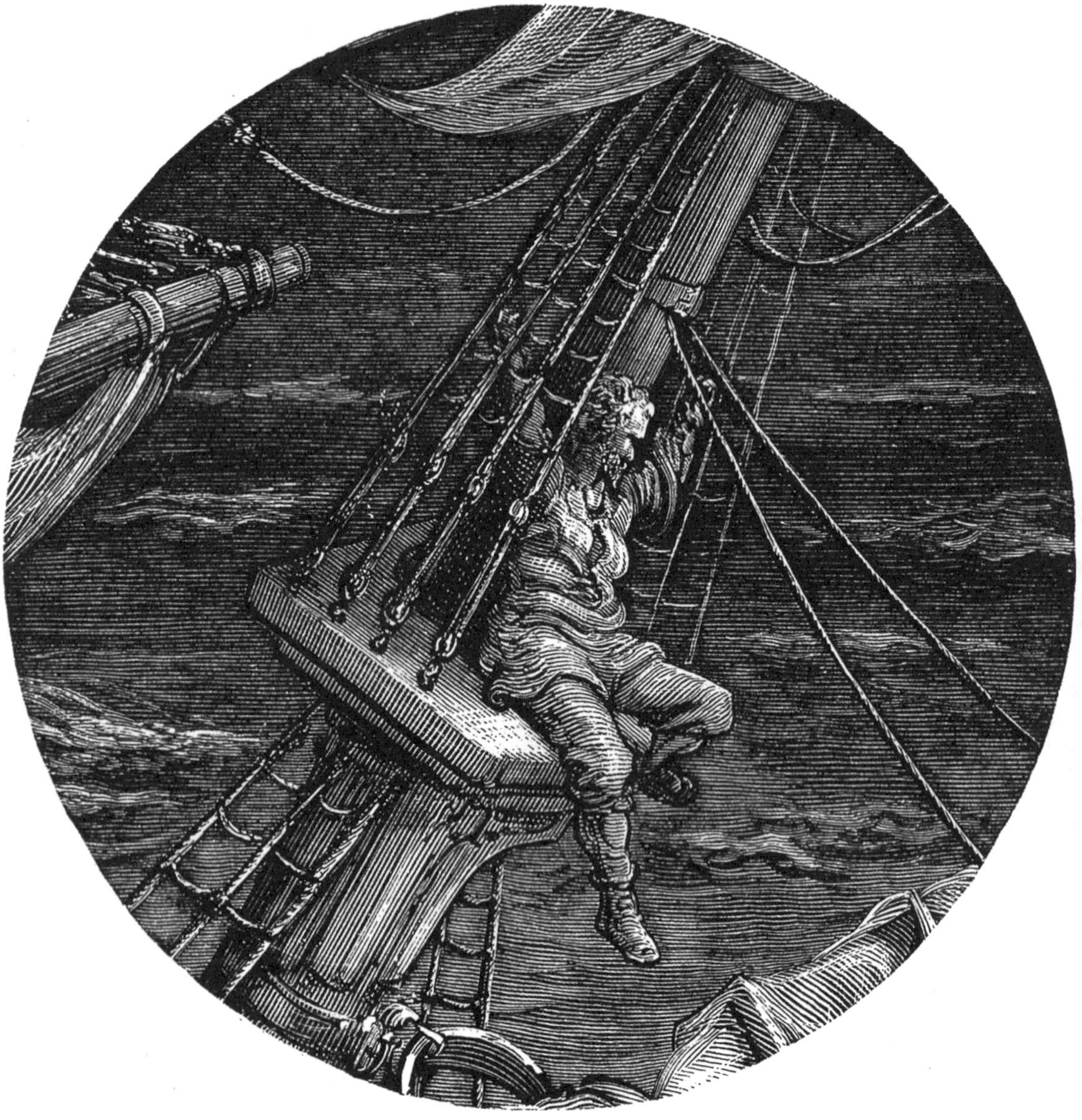

Part One
第一部分

IT is an ancient Mariner,
And he stoppeth one of three.
"By thy long grey beard and glittering eye,
Now wherefore stopp'st thou me?

那是一个老年舟子,
三人中拦住一人。
"目光炯炯的这老汉,
你拦我为甚原因?

An ancient Mariner meeteth three Gallants bidden to a wedding-feast, and detaineth one.
一位老年舟子遇到三位要去参加婚礼宴会的时髦青年男子,并拉住其中一位。

The Bridegroom's doors are opened wide,
And I am next of kin;
The guests are met, the feast is set:
May'st hear the merry din."

新郎家前大门洞启,
我最亲被召婚筵。
宾客到齐,排了酒席——
听那边笑语喧阗。"

He holds him with his skinny hand,

"There was a ship," quoth he.

"Hold off! unhand me, grey-beard loon!"

Eftsoons his hand dropt he.

他用如柴手掌抓住：

"我当初在一舟中——"

"站开！放手，羊须老汉！"

他闻言立刻手松。

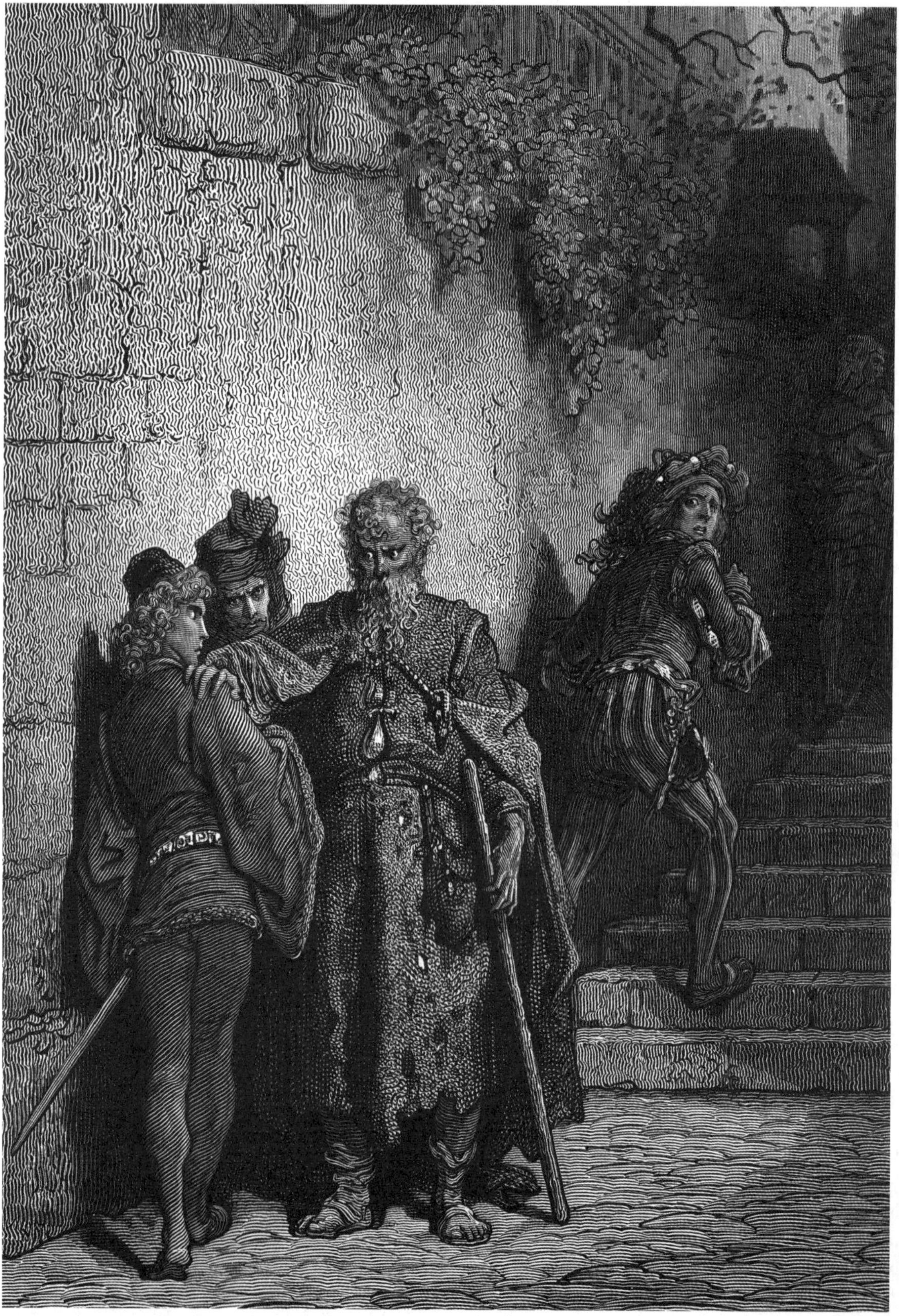

He holds him with his glittering eye-
The Wedding-Guest stood still,
And listens like a three years' child:
The Mariner hath his will.

The Wedding-Guest sat on a stone:
He cannot choose but hear;
And thus spake on that ancient man,
The bright-eyed Mariner.

但他双眼有如磁铁,
令喜宾不得不留,
在路旁,靠石头坐下,
听老人述说根由。

The Wedding-Guest is spellbound by the eye of the old seafaring man, and constrained to hear his tale.
赴宴的宾客被老舟子的眼睛震慑住了,不得不听他的故事。

"The ship was cheered, the harbour cleared,
Merrily did we drop
Below the kirk, below the hill,
Below the lighthouse top.

"船拔锚碇离开泊岸,
行驶过庄严教堂,
旋出罗盘似的山影,
越灯塔,到水中央。

The Sun came up upon the left,
Out of the sea came he!
And he shone bright, and on the right
Went down into the sea.

日头在水左方升上,
过苍苍似是孤帆。
他待长庚出来时候,
向右方掷下金丸。

The Mariner tells how the ship sailed southward with a good wind and fair weather, till it reached the line.
老舟子讲述船是如何在一个极好的风向和晴朗的天气里起航的,直到他们到达海岸线。

Higher and higher every day,
Till over the mast at noon—"
The Wedding-Guest here beat his breast,
For he heard the loud bassoon.

一天过去高似一天，
直到交午桅杆上——"
喜宾急得双手捶胸，
因他闻笛声嘹亮。

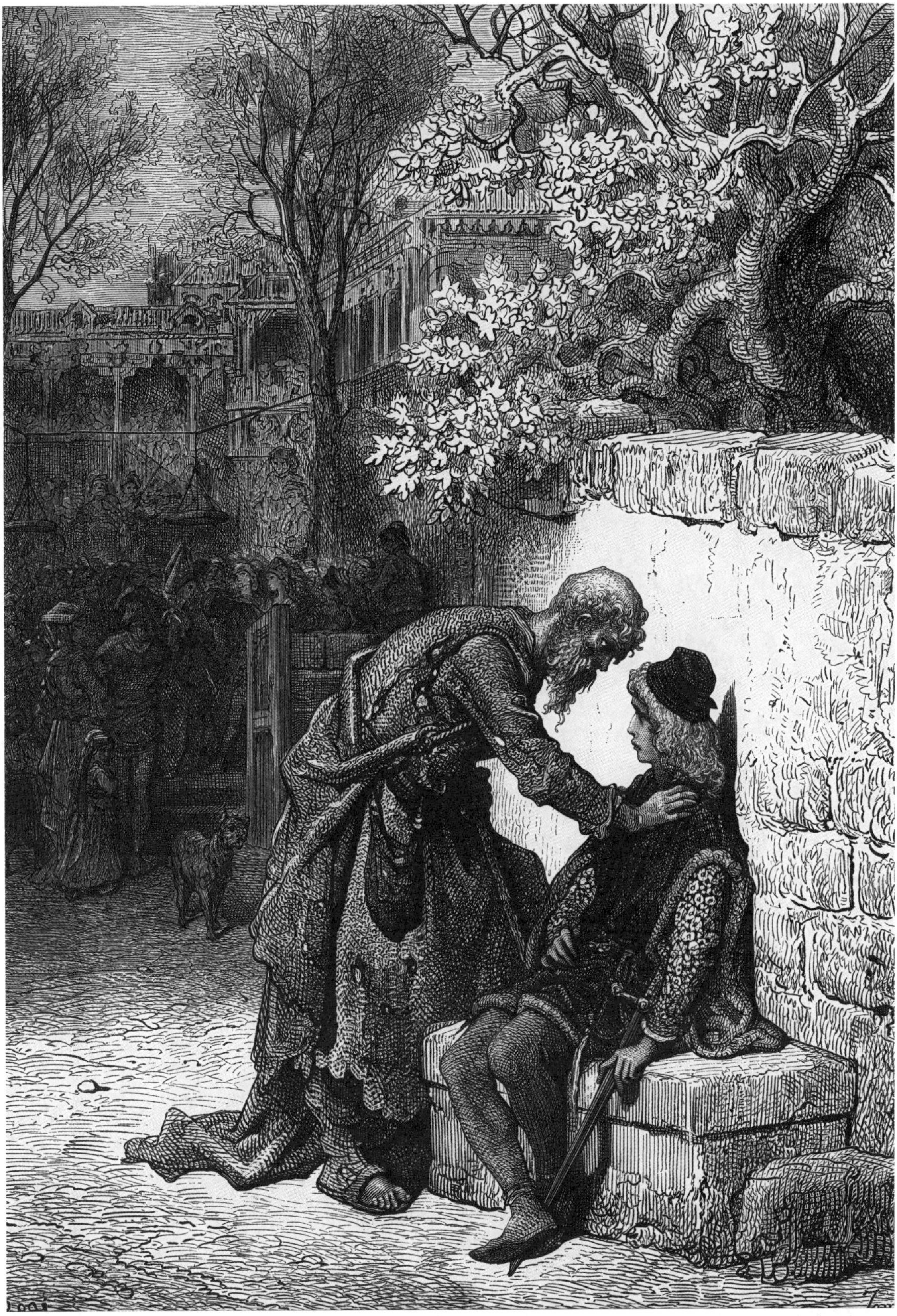

The bride hath paced into the hall,
Red as a rose is she;
Nodding their heads before her goes
The merry minstrelsy.

新妇已经步到堂上，
脸绯红好像蔷薇。
在她前面，鼓腮点首，
乐师将箫管高吹。

The Wedding-Guest heareth the bridal music; but the Mariner continueth his tale.
赴宴的宾客听着婚礼的音乐，而舟子还在继续着他的故事。

The Wedding-Guest he beat his breast,
Yet he cannot choose but hear;
And thus spake on that ancient man,
The bright-eyed Mariner.

喜宾急得捶胸搓掌,
但他仍不得不留
在路旁,靠石头坐下,
听老人续述根由。

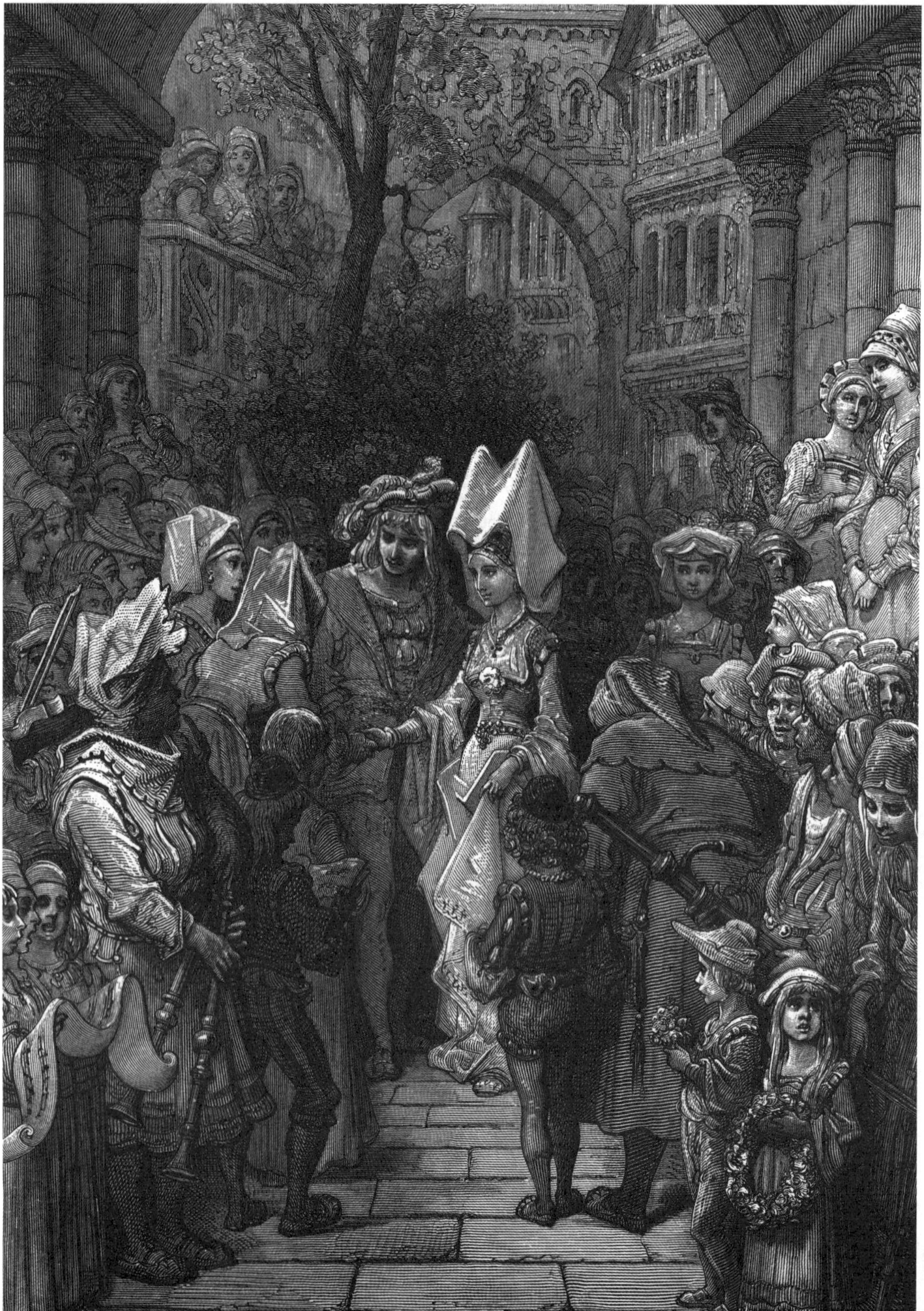

"And now the STORM-BLAST came,
And he was tyrannous and strong:
He struck with his o'ertaking wings,
And chased us south along.

"忽然风暴卷起洋面,
万里中但见洪波,
我们的船向南刮去,
舟中人徒唤奈何。

The ship drawn by a storm toward the south pole.
船被风暴赶向南极。

With sloping masts and dipping prow,
As who pursued with yell and blow
Still treads the shadow of his foe,
And forward bends his head,
The ship drove fast, loud roared the blast,
And southward aye we fled.

樯倾斜着，首没水中，
如巨人低头追敌，
我们的船，破浪乘风，
向南奔一时不息。

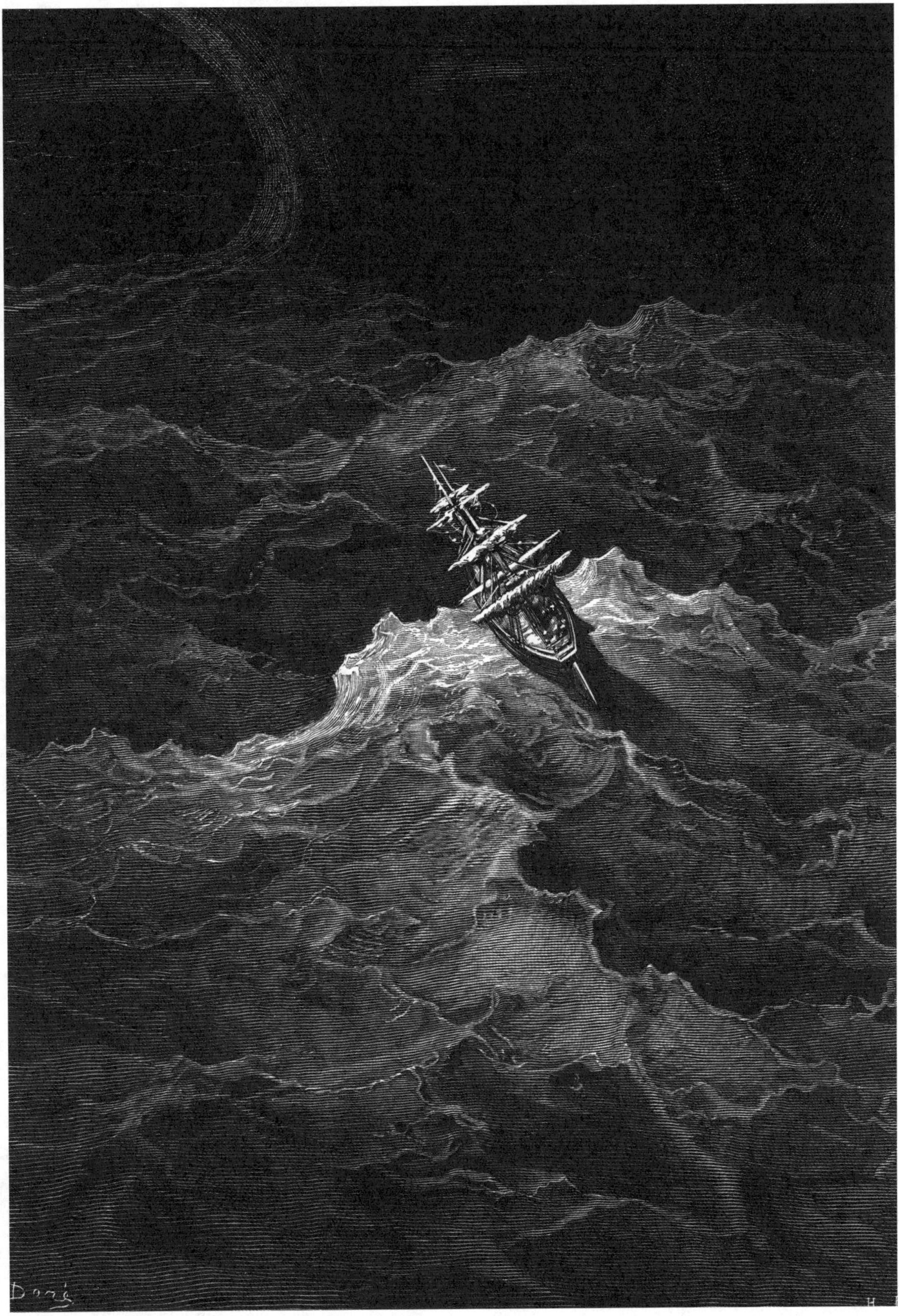
Doré

And now there came both mist and snow,
And it grew wondrous cold:
And ice, mast-high, came floating by,
As green as emerald.

我们驶入雾同白雪,
地峭寒不可留停,
桅杆高的冰山漂过,
翡翠般碧绿晶莹。

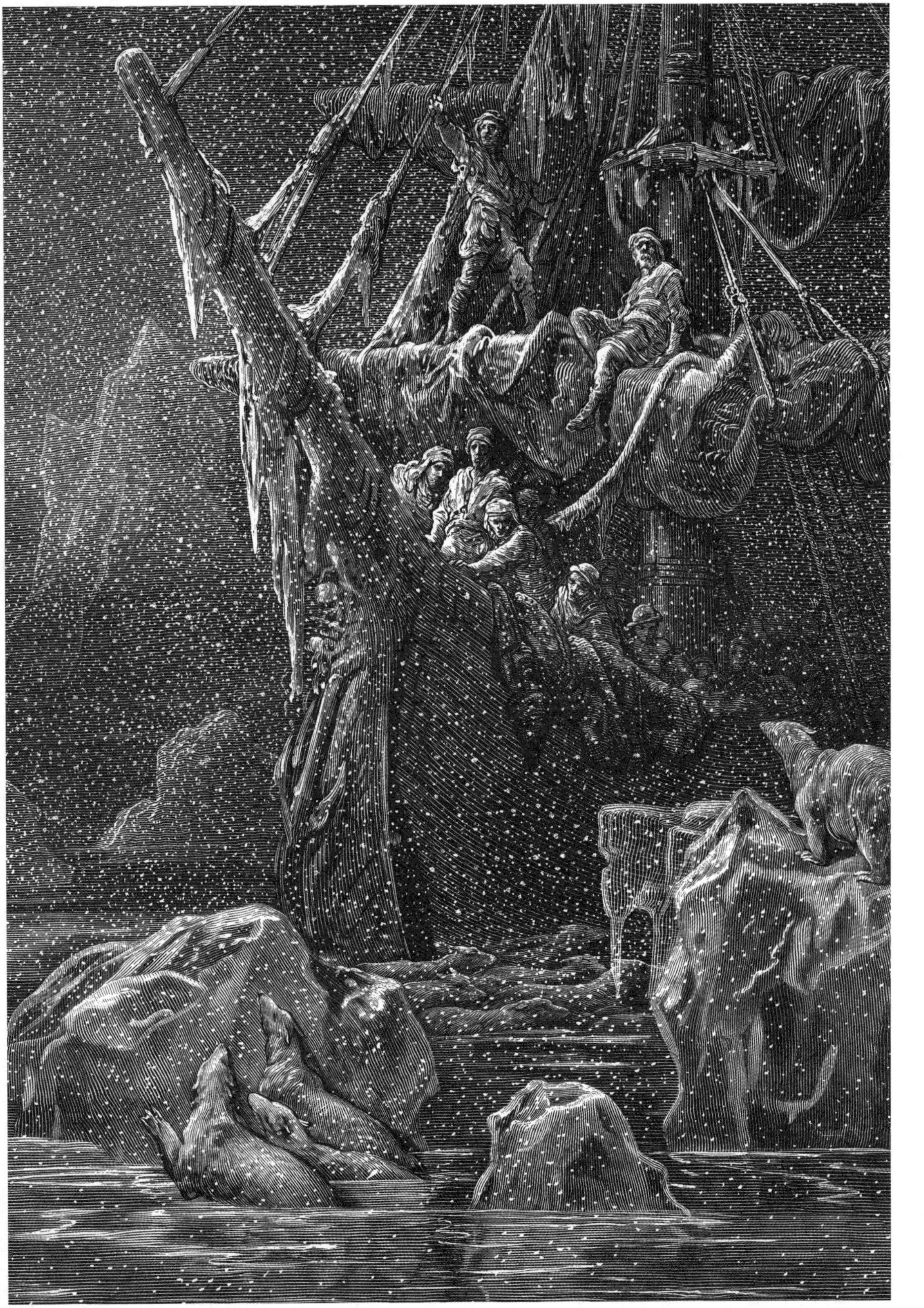

And through the drifts the snowy clifts
Did send a dismal sheen:
Nor shapes of men nor beasts we ken—
The ice was all between.

浮冰之间尚多雪岭,
射过来惨淡光辉,
不见人影,亦无兽迹——
只坚冰环绕周围。

The land of ice, and of fearful sounds where no living thing was to be seen.
结冰的陆地和着可怕的声音,到处看不到生命的迹象。

The ice was here, the ice was there,

The ice was all around:

It cracked and growled, and roared and howled,

Like noises in a swound!

航过一程还是冰岛,

更航行晶岭当前:

它们毕剥,喧豗,澎湃,

如晕时声震耳边!

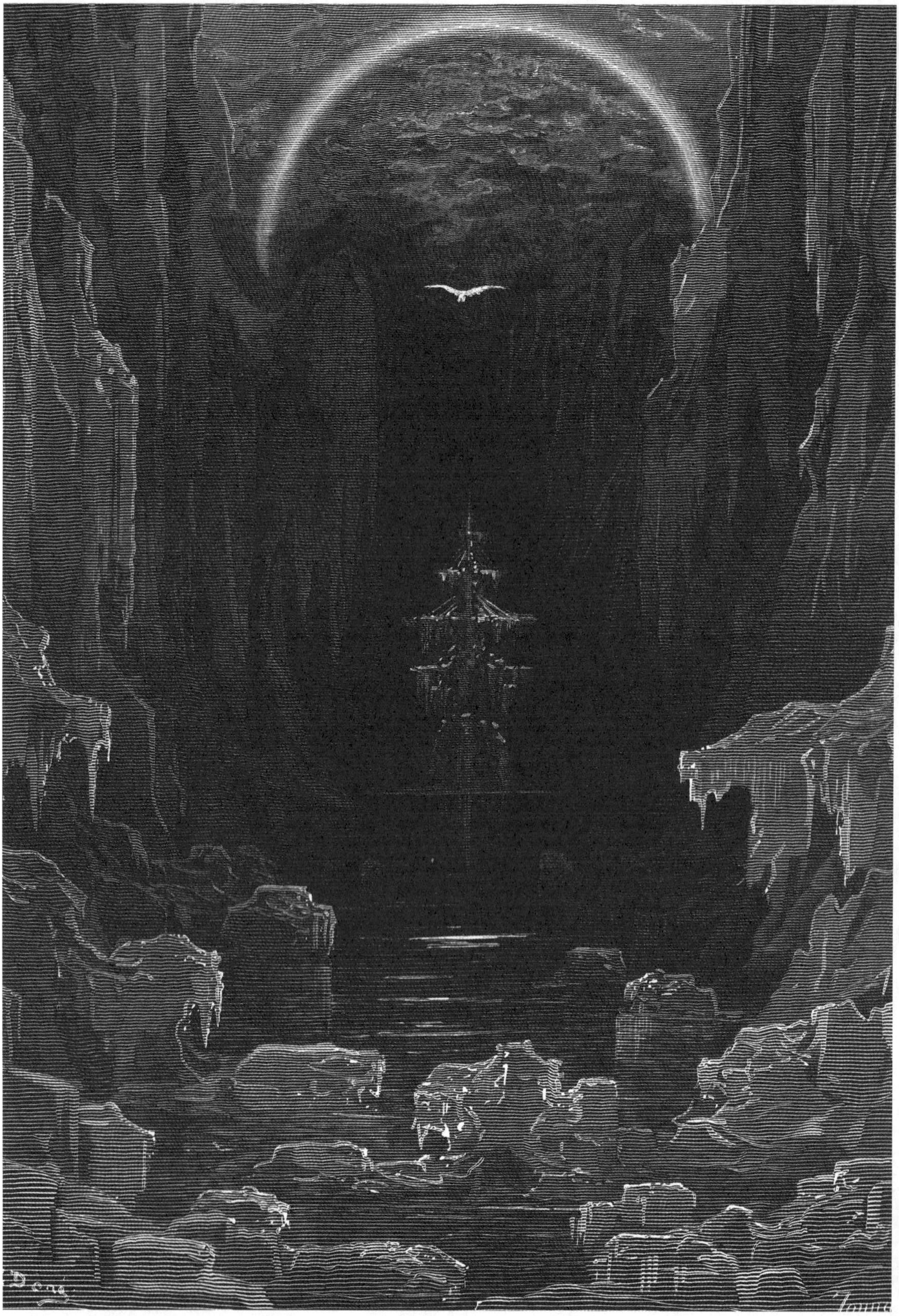

At length did cross an Albatross,
Thorough the fog it came;
As if it had been a Christian soul,
We hailed it in God's name.

有一海燕穿过浓雾，
它向船冉冉飞来。
我们见它似逢故友，
拍手呼，乐满胸怀。

Till a great seabird, called the Albatross, came through the snow-fog, and was received with great joy and hospitality.
直到一只名为海燕的海鸟，穿过雪雾而来，船员们带着极大的欢喜和热情好客迎接它的降落。

It ate the food it ne'er had eat,
And round and round it flew.
The ice did split with a thunder-fit;
The helmsman steered us through!

我们取食充它饥腹,
它在空反复翱翔。
冰山忽爆,舵工取道
载我们逃出中央!

And a good south wind sprung up behind;
The Albatross did follow,
And every day, for food or play,
Came to the mariners' hollo!

起了南风，吹舟北上，
后方那海燕紧跟，
每天取食，或是玩耍，
闻呼即来临！

And lo! the Albatross proveth a bird of good omen, and followeth the ship as it returned northward through fog and floating ice.
看！海燕飞来是个好兆头，它随着船只穿过雪雾和流动的冰掉头北返。

In mist or cloud, on mast or shroud,
It perched for vespers nine;
Whiles all the night, through fog-smoke white,
Glimmered the white Moon-shine."

雾里，云中，樯头，帆上，
它总共停了九天；
这九天内，穿过浓雾，
有月光亮在夜间。"

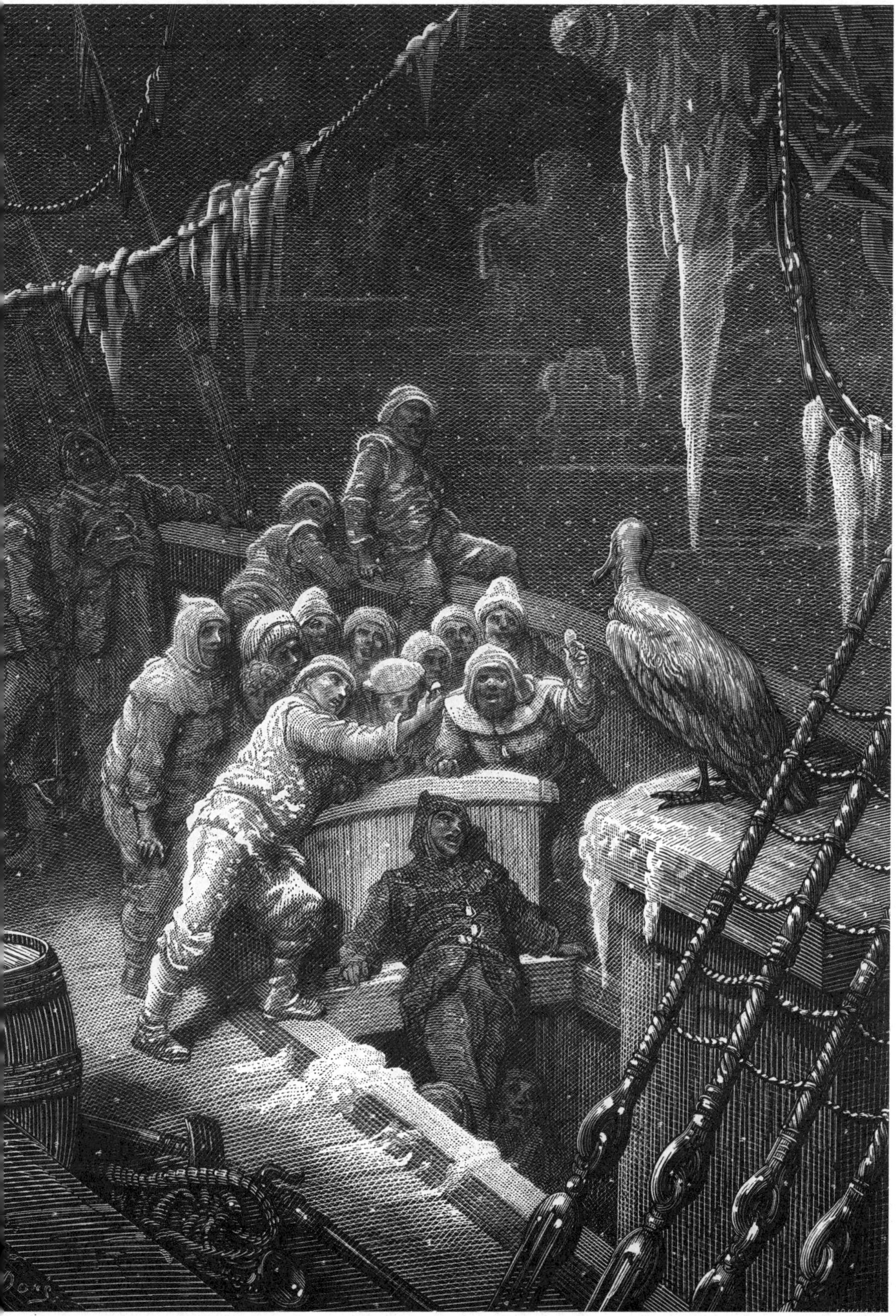

"God save thee, ancient Mariner!
From the fiends, that plague thee thus!—
Why look'st thou so?" — "With my cross-bow
I shot the ALBATROSS."

"你的双目何以发光,
如魔鬼附身,舟子?
天保佑你!"——"是我弯弓
一箭将海燕射死!"

The ancient Mariner inhospitably killeth the pious bird of good omen.
年老的舟子无情地杀死了善良而真诚的吉鸟。

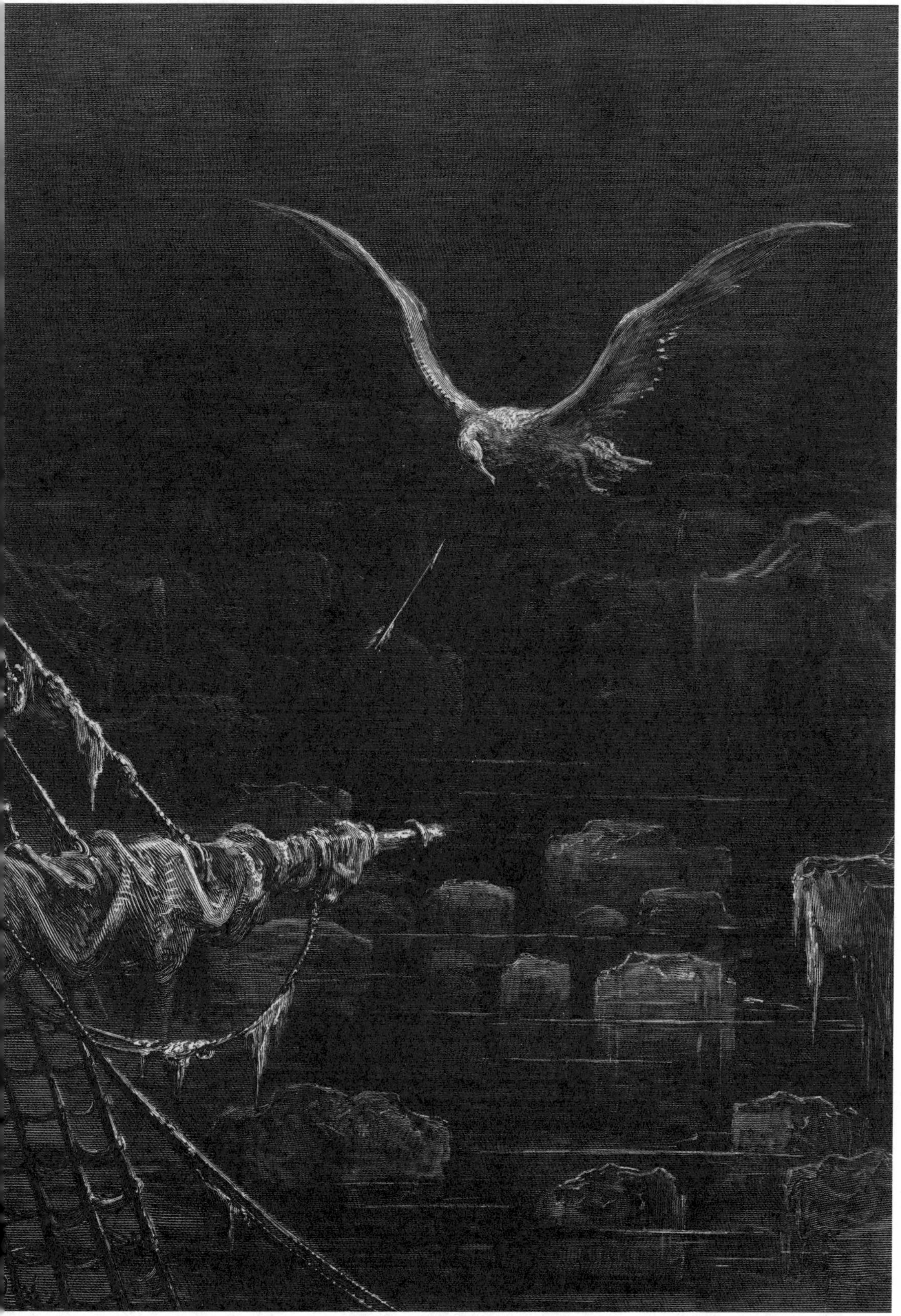

Part Two

第二部分

"THE Sun now rose upon the right:
Out of the sea came he,
Still hid in mist, and on the left
Went down into the sea.

"日头自水右方升上,
隔雾瞧好像银丸,
它落寞地奔驰一日,
在左方落下波澜。

And the good south wind still blew behind,
But no sweet bird did follow,
Nor any day for food or play
Came to the mariners' hollo!

南风依旧吹舟北上,
但后方无鸟紧跟,
每天取食,或是玩耍,
闻吆喝即便来临!

And I had done a hellish thing,
And it would work 'em woe:
For all averred, I had killed the bird
That made the breeze to blow.
'Ah wretch!' said they, 'the bird to slay,
That made the breeze to blow!'

事情是我一人做错，
祸来将连累人家。
他们责我不该杀鸟，
因风生全是为它。

His shipmates cry out against the ancient Mariner, for killing the bird of good luck.
船友们大声斥责老舟子，因为他射死了幸运之鸟。

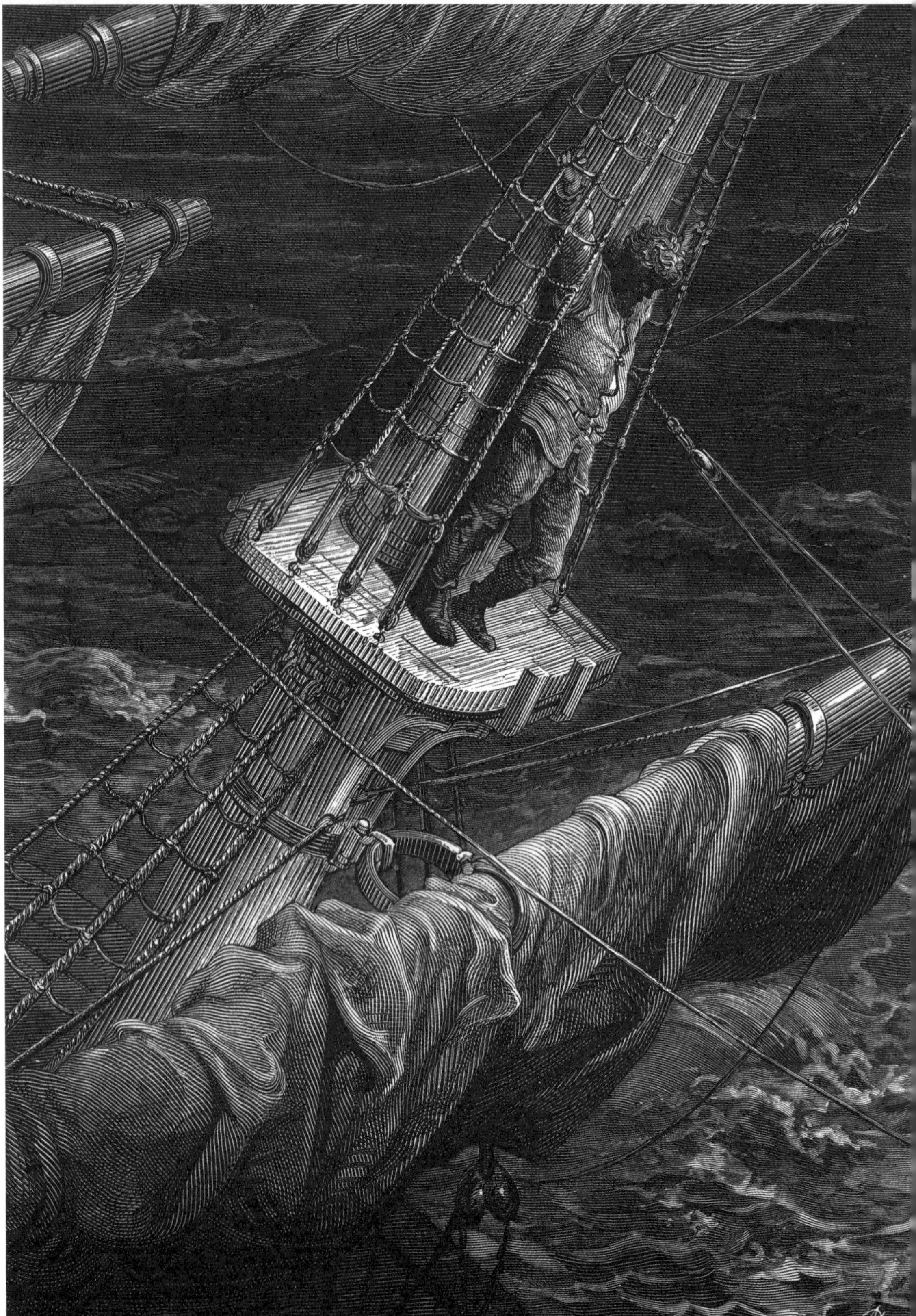

Nor dim nor red, like God's own head,
The glorious Sun uprist:
Then all averred, I had killed the bird
That brought the fog and mist.
''Twas right,' said they, 'such birds to slay,
That bring the fog and mist.'

哪知次日太阳灿烂，
无纤云点染苍穹——
他们说，这凶鸟该杀，
是为它雾气漫空。

But when the fog cleared off, they justify the same, and thus make themselves accomplices in the crime.
可当迷雾散去，他们又一致改口为老舟子辩护，从而让自己成为帮凶。

The fair breeze blew, the white foam flew,
The furrow followed free;
We were the first that ever burst
Into that silent sea.

拂拂风吹，浪花纷飞，
舟迹随有如燕尾；
以往无人，唯有我们
第一次航行此水。

The fair breeze continues; the ship enters the Pacific Ocean, and sails northward, even till it reaches the line.
和风继续吹着；船航行进太平洋，向北起航，抵达赤道后也未转向。

Down dropt the breeze, the sails dropt down,
'Twas sad as sad could be;
And we did speak only to break
The silence of the sea!

圆的布篷忽然瘪下，
风飔已迹灭形销；
悄然不闻波吻船首，
或狂澜奔突呼嚣。

The ship hath been suddenly becalmed.
船突然停止前进。

All in a hot and copper sky,
The bloody Sun, at noon,
Right up above the mast did stand,
No bigger than the Moon.

赤铜色的亢暑天上，
血样红一轮太阳，
它大小与圆月相仿，
交午时正对帆樯。

Day after day, day after day,
We stuck, nor breath nor motion;
As idle as a painted ship
Upon a painted ocean.

一天接着一天过去，
无风来作浪推舟，
它像一条画的船舶
停在画的海上头。

Water, water, every where,
And all the boards did shrink;
Water, water, every where,
Nor any drop to drink.

这边是水，那边是水，
但船板干得裂开；
这边是水，那边是水，
无饮水滋润心怀。

And the Albatross begins to be avenged.
海燕开始复仇。

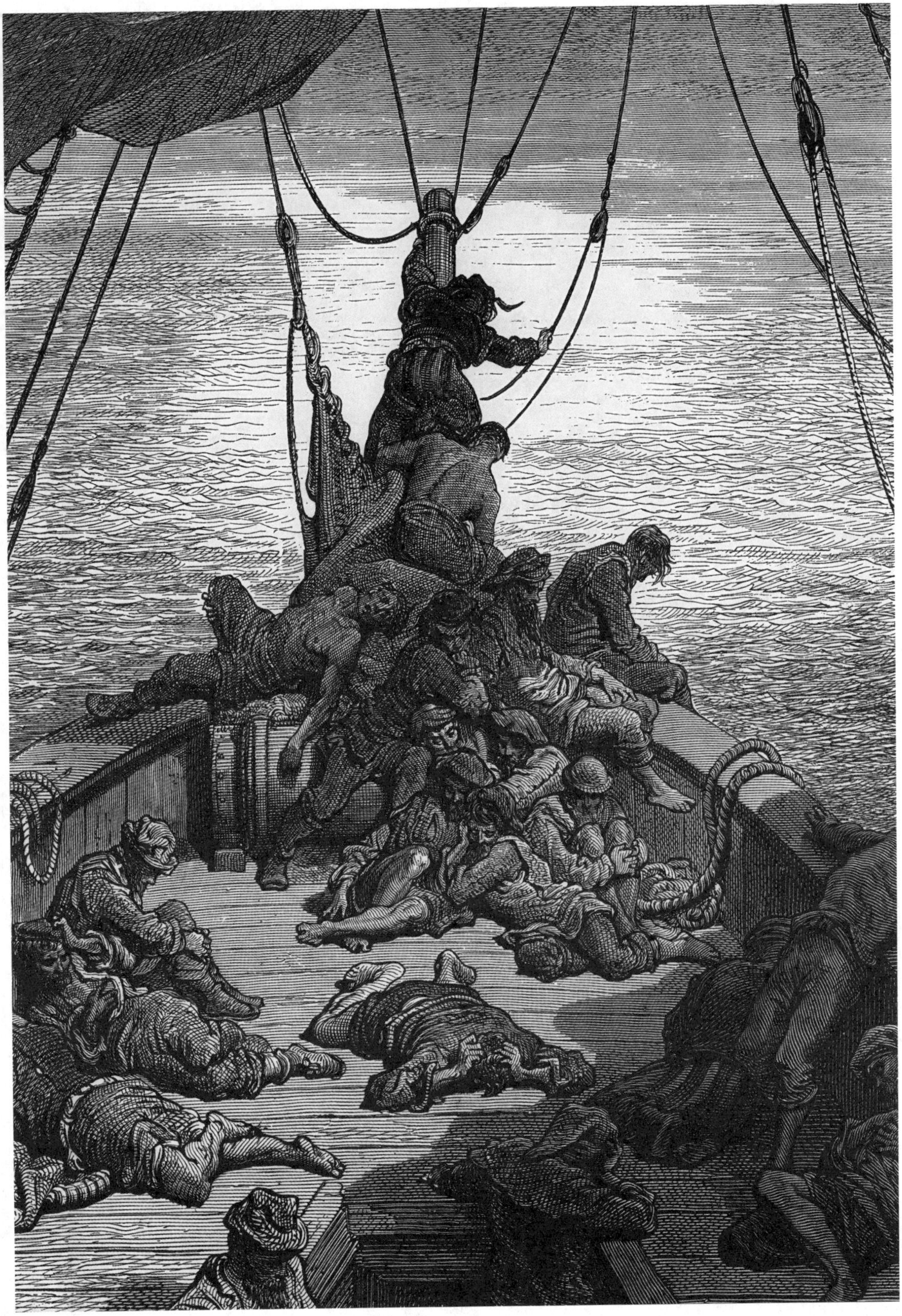

The very deep did rot: O Christ!
That ever this should be!
Yea, slimy things did crawl with legs
Upon the slimy sea.

连海都霉烂了，基督！
这真是骇人听闻！
你瞧，在那污湿水面，
污湿的虫豸爬行。

About, about, in reel and rout,
The death-fires danced at night;
The water, like a witch's oils,
Burnt green, and blue and white.

时前时后,时左时右,
是死火狂舞夜间;
青的洋水变红转白,
如妖巫锅内油煎。

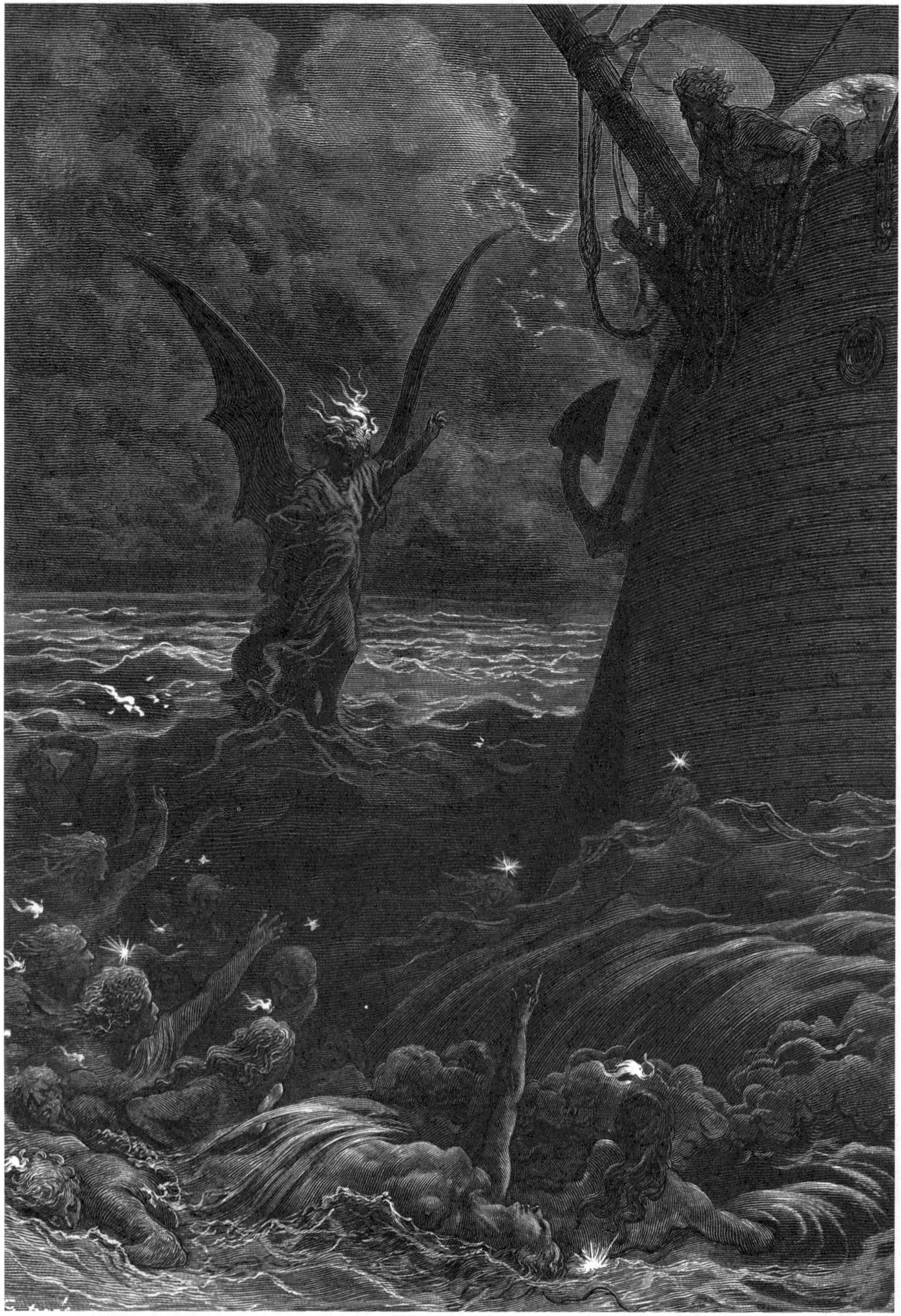

And some in dreams assured were
Of the Spirit that plagued us so;
Nine fathom deep he had followed us
From the land of mist and snow.

有人梦内得到兆示，
知是一神道相磨；
他自南极雪霜之地
随了来，潜伏洪波。

A spirit had followed them; one of the invisible inhabitants of this planet, neither departed souls nor angels; concerning whom the learned Jew, Josephus, and the Platonic Constantinopolitan, Michael Psellus, may be consulted. They are very numerous, and there is no climate or element without one or more.

一个幽灵跟着他们，那是一种在这个星球上看不见的、不是鬼魂也不是天使的生命；博学的犹太人约瑟夫斯和君士坦丁堡的柏拉图式主义者迈克·塞勒斯也许知道有关这个幽灵的信息。他们数量浩如繁星，没有一个地方不充斥着他们的身影。

And every tongue, through utter drought,

Was withered at the root;

We could not speak, no more than if

We had been choked with soot.

许久不曾滴水沾口，

舌根直干到尖头；

我们渴得不能说话，

如丸泥封起咽喉。

Ah! well-a-day! what evil looks
Had I from old and young!
Instead of the cross, the Albatross
About my neck was hung."

唉！他们内无分老少，
见我都怒目攒眉！
他们解去银十字架，
拿鸟在我颈悬垂。"

The shipmates, in their sore distress, would fain throw the whole guilt on the ancient Mariner: in sign whereof they hang the dead sea-bird round his neck.
沉浸在悲痛中的水手们，终会欣然地把愧疚归在老舟子的身上：因为他们把那死去的海燕挂在老舟子的颈间，以示咎责。

Part Three
第三部分

"THERE passed a weary time. Each throat
Was parched, and glazed each eye.
A weary time! a weary time!
How glazed each weary eye,
When looking westward, I beheld
A something in the sky.

"双目死鱼一样瞪视,
双唇已龟裂焦黄。
我无意中四周游目,
见一物来自西方。

The ancient Mariner beholdeth a sign in the element afar off.
老舟子看到远处好像有什么东西来了。

At first it seemed a little speck,
And then it seemed a mist;
It moved and moved, and took at last
A certain shape, I wist.

骤看有如小的斑点,
再看时又似轻烟——
它向此船渐渐行近,
自茫茫天的那边。

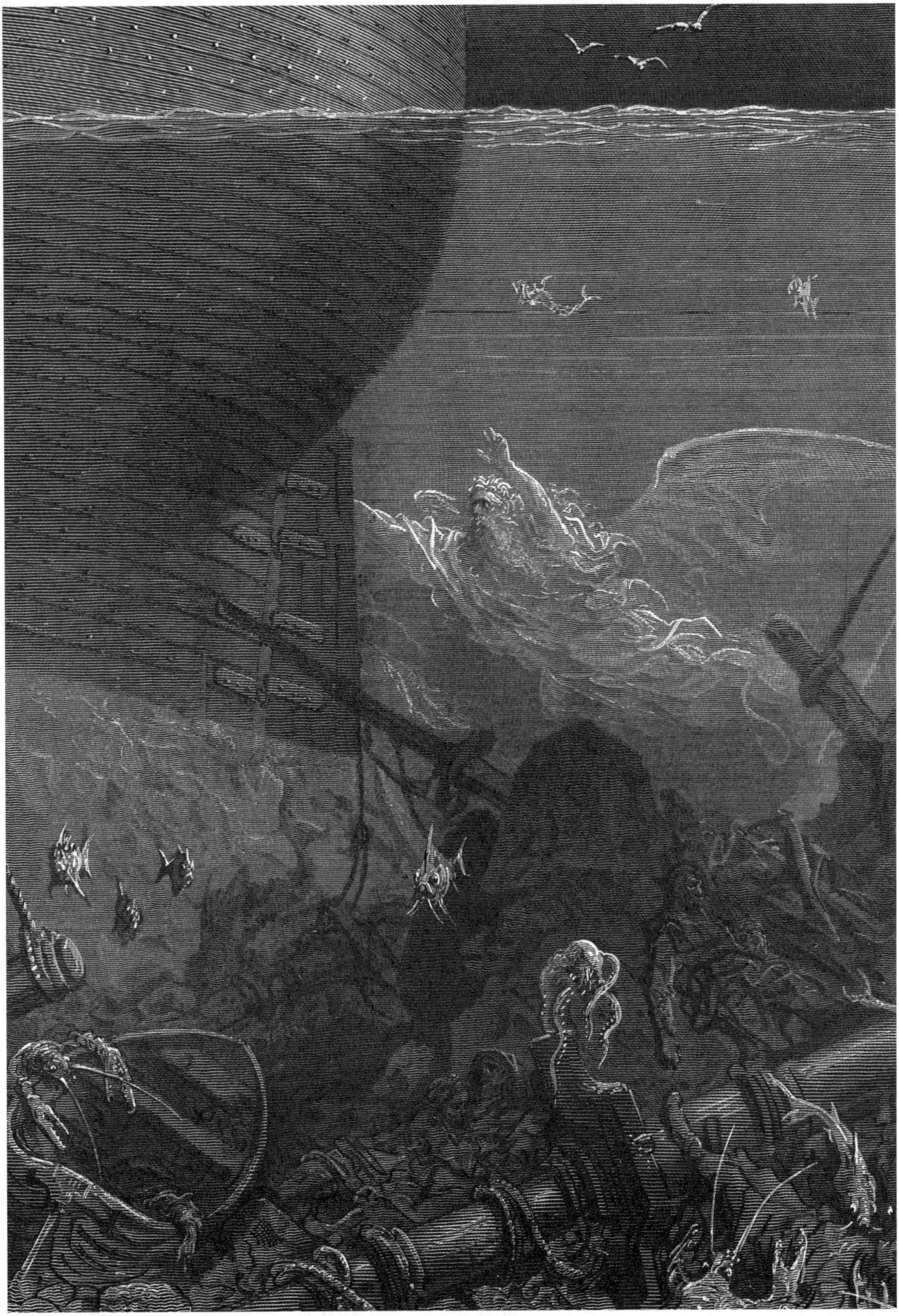

A speck, a mist, a shape, I wist!
And still it neared and neared:
As if it dodged a water-sprite,
It plunged and tacked and veered.

既肖轻烟，又如斑点，
它愈行愈近我们。
它蝴蝶般刻左刻右，
如躲避海里妖精。

With throats unslaked, with black lips baked,
We could nor laugh nor wail;
Through utter drought all dumb we stood!
I bit my arm, I sucked the blood,
And cried, A sail! a sail!

咽喉干涸,嘴唇焦黑,
欲笑啼气皆不通!
我咬臂膀,吞下鲜血,
才叫出,船篷!船篷!

At its nearer approach, it seemeth him to be a ship; and at a dear ransom he freeth his speech from the bonds of thirst.
随着它不断地逼近,他似乎看到了一艘船。他从干渴中大喊出来。

With throats unslaked, with black lips baked,
Agape they heard me call:
Gramercy! they for joy did grin,
And all at once their breath drew in,
As they were drinking all.

咽喉干涸,嘴唇噍黑,
张着口听我高呼,
他们乐得尽是咧嘴,
齐吸气如饮醍醐。

A flash of joy;
顷刻间喜笑颜开。

See! see! (I cried) she tacks no more!
Hither to work us weal;
Without a breeze, without a tide,
She steadies with upright keel!

看！我呼道，看它径进
来此将我们救援；
不对！没有风与潮汐，
它怎的行过波澜？

And horror follows. For can it be a ship that comes onward without wind or tide?
恐惧随之而来，没有风浪，它怎能直挺挺地行进？

The western wave was all a-flame,
The day was well nigh done!
Almost upon the western wave
Rested the broad bright Sun;
When that strange shape drove suddenly
Betwixt us and the Sun.

西方波浪有如焰火，
擎托着大的太阳，
那条船舶忽然航进
我们与日的中央。

And straight the Sun was flecked with bars,
(Heaven's Mother send us grace!)
As if through a dungeon-grate he peered
With broad and burning face.

太阳形状立刻改变，
（天哪，那多么骇人！）
它像拿了炽热之面
紧贴在牢狱栅门。

It seemeth him but the skeleton of a ship.
在他看来，那船只只有骨架了。

Alas! (thought I, and my heart beat loud)
How fast she nears and nears!
Are those her sails that glance in the Sun,
Like restless gossameres?

我的心在胸口乱跳,
因她来疾速如飞!
那可是她帆上之布,
似游丝吹去吹回?

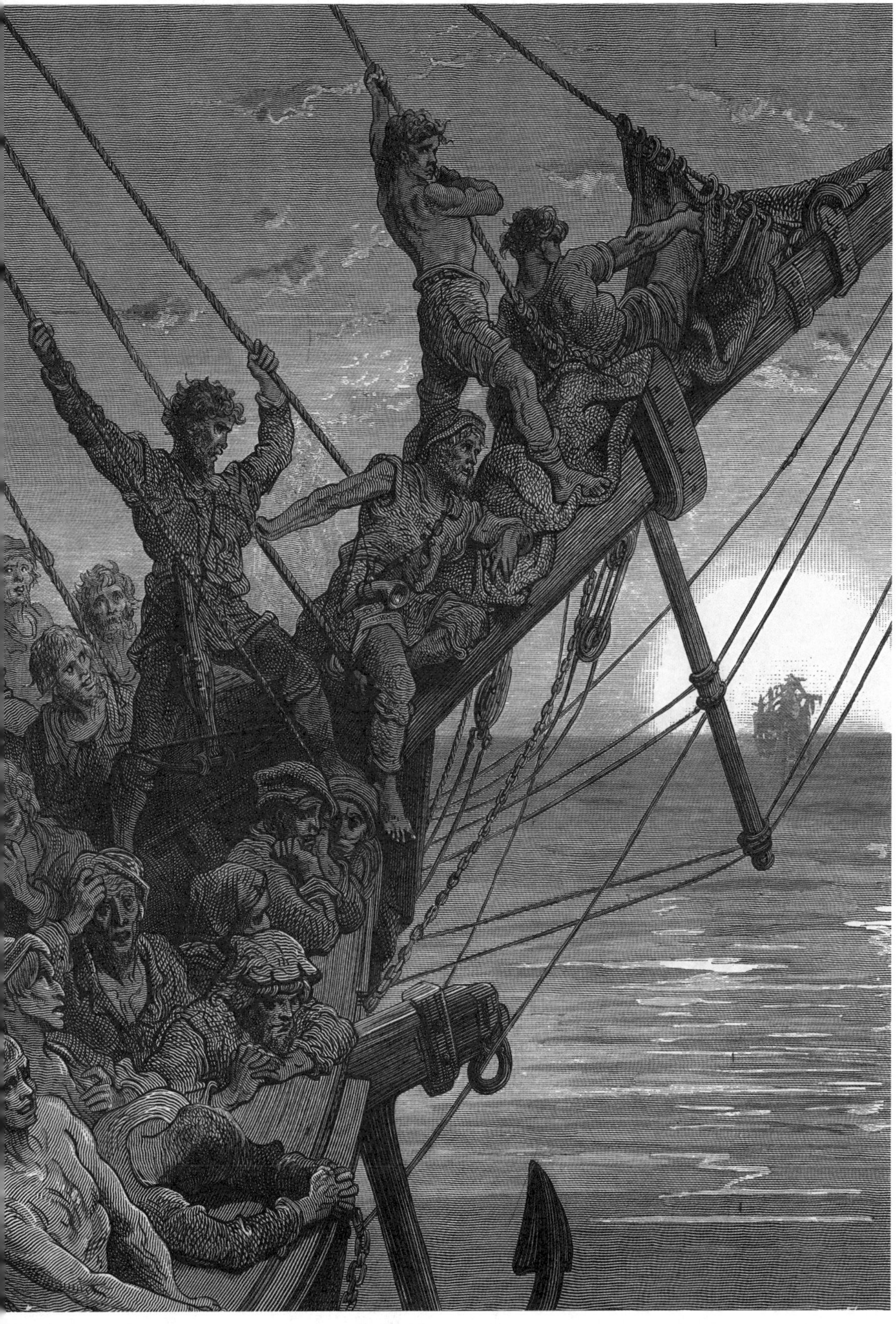

Are those her ribs through which the Sun

Did peer, as through a grate?

And is that Woman all her crew?

Is that a DEATH? and are there two?

Is DEATH that Woman's mate?

那些可是她的肋骨,

如铁栏遮住太阳?

船上只有那个妖妇?

伴她的可是死亡?

And its ribs are seen as bars on the face of the setting Sun.
The Spectre-Woman and her Death-mate, and no other, on board the skeleton-ship.

它的肋骨像铁栏一样挡住太阳。

骨架上只有妖女和她的"死"的同僚还在甲板上。

Her lips were red, her looks were free,
Her locks were yellow as gold:
Her skin was as white as leprosy,
The Nightmare LIFE-IN-DEATH was she,
Who thicks man's blood with cold.

唇如血染，头发土黄：
皮肤白似癣遮身。
死之生是她的名字，
人听到便打寒噤。

like vessel, like crew!
船啊，船员啊！

The naked hulk alongside came,
And the twain were casting dice;
'The game is done! I've won, I've won!'
Quoth she, and whistles thrice.

那船到了我们身侧，
两人正掷骰呼卢。
'赌赛完毕，我已胜利！'
她说时撮口三呼。

Death and Life-in-Death have diced for the ship's crew, and she (the latter) winneth the ancient Mariner.
"死"与"死之生"为全体船员的命运掷骰子，最后，她（后者）赢了老水手。

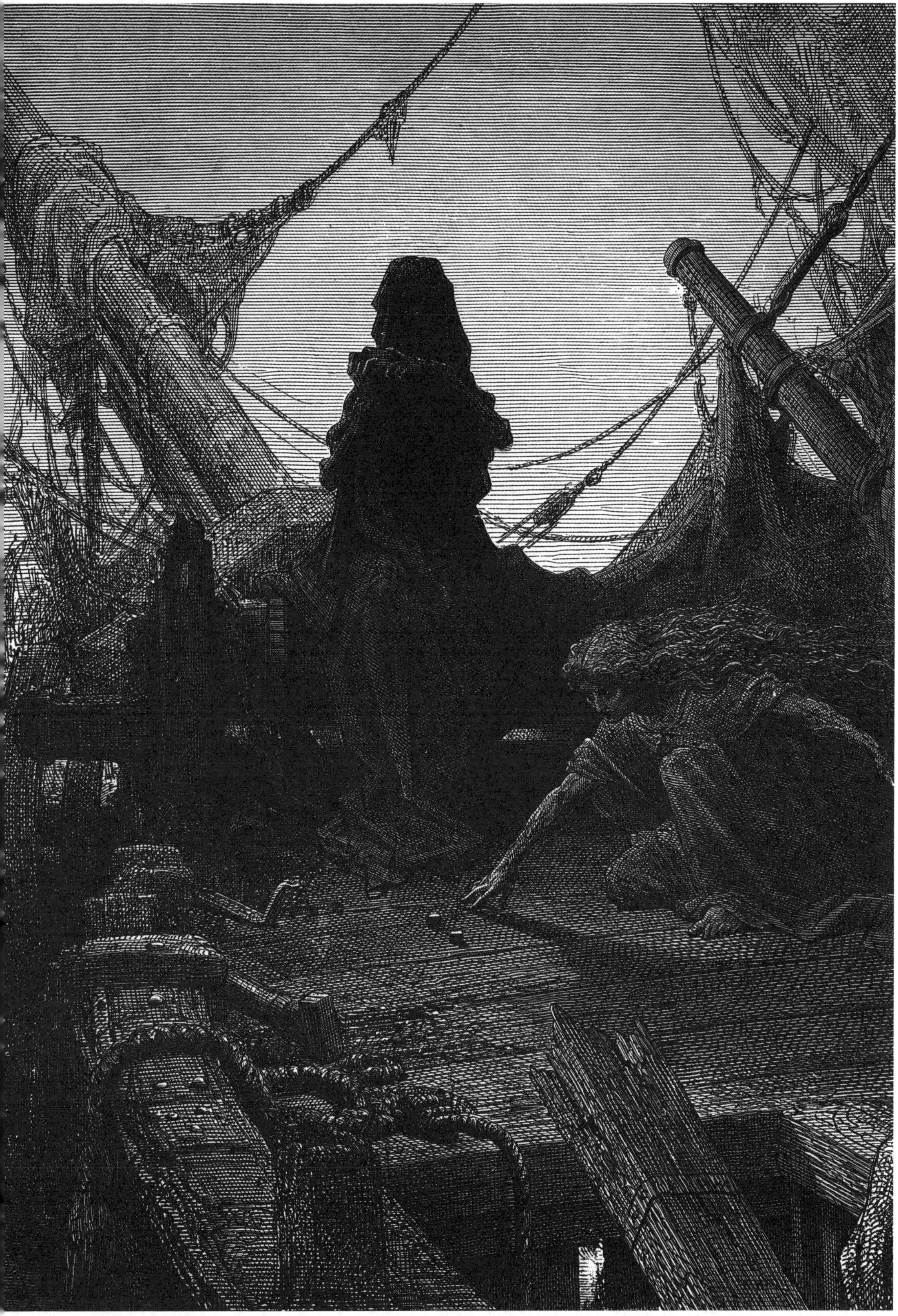

The Sun's rim dips; the stars rush out:
At one stride comes the dark;
With far-heard whisper, o'er the sea,
Off shot the spectre-bark.

日落，众星同时跳出：
转眼间黑暗弥空。
有如羽箭激气作响，
那鬼舟射出望中。

No twilight within the courts of the Sun.
海天之间，暮色已尽。

We listened and looked sideways up!

Fear at my heart, as at a cup,

My life-blood seemed to sip!

The stars were dim, and thick the night,

The steersman's face by his lamp gleamed white;

From the sails the dew did drip—

Till clomb above the eastern bar

The horned Moon, with one bright star

Within the nether tip.

灯光照见舵工苍白,
露水时滴下布帆,
一钩黄月自东钻出,
将孤星钳在下端。

At the rising of the Moon,
一轮明月升起,

One after one, by the star-dogged Moon,
Too quick for groan or sigh,
Each turned his face with a ghastly pang,
And cursed me with his eye.

在月亮的昏黄光下，
他们受剧痛扭身，
来不及呻吟，或叹息，
但恚恨充溢眼睛。

One after another,
一个接着一个，

Four times fifty living men
(And I heard nor sigh nor groan),
With heavy thump, a lifeless lump,
They dropped down one by one.

他们默然将我诅咒——
接连着尸倒船头。
只听船板碰得连响,
二百人无一存留。

His shipmates drop down dead;
同船的船员们倒地身亡。

The souls did from their bodies fly, —
They fled to bliss or woe!
And every soul, it passed me by,
Like the whizz of my cross-bow!"

他们魂魄离开尸首——
阻重洋能返家园？——
离时魂魄簌簌作响，
如我的弩箭辞弦！"

But Life-in-Death begins her work on the ancient Mariner.
但是"死之生"保住了老水手的性命。

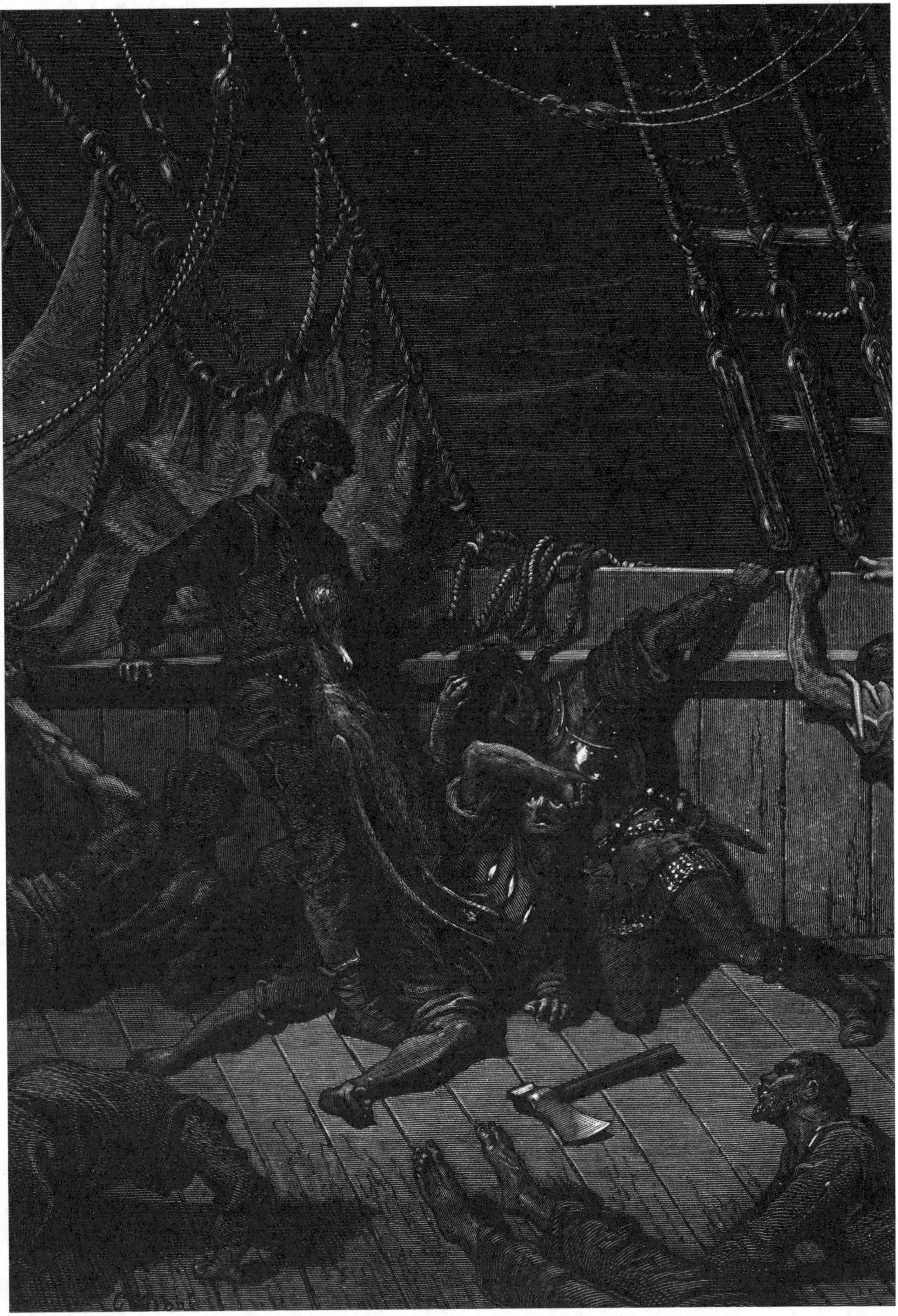

Part Four
第四部分

"I FEAR thee, ancient Mariner!
I fear thy skinny hand!
And thou art long, and lank, and brown,
As is the ribbed sea-sand.

"我怕你呀,老年舟子!
我怕你手似枯柴!
你的伙伴皆已死尽,
你怎能活着归来?

The Wedding-Guest feareth that a Spirit is talking to him;
婚宴的宾客害怕是一个幽灵在和他说话。

I fear thee and thy glittering eye,
And thy skinny hand, so brown."—
"Fear not, fear not, thou Wedding-Guest!
This body dropt not down.

我怕你那异光双眼，
我怕你瘦手盘筋。"——
"不要怕呀，我未倒下，
你身边这是生人。

Alone, alone, all, all alone,
Alone on a wide wide sea!
And never a saint took pity on
My soul in agony.

孤零零的，无人做伴，
孤零地在海中间，
任我若何呼天抢地，
神祇中无一垂怜。

But the ancient Mariner assureth him of his bodily life, and proceedeth to relate his horrible penance.
但老舟子使宾客相信他是真实存在的，又继续讲述他骇人听闻的忏悔。

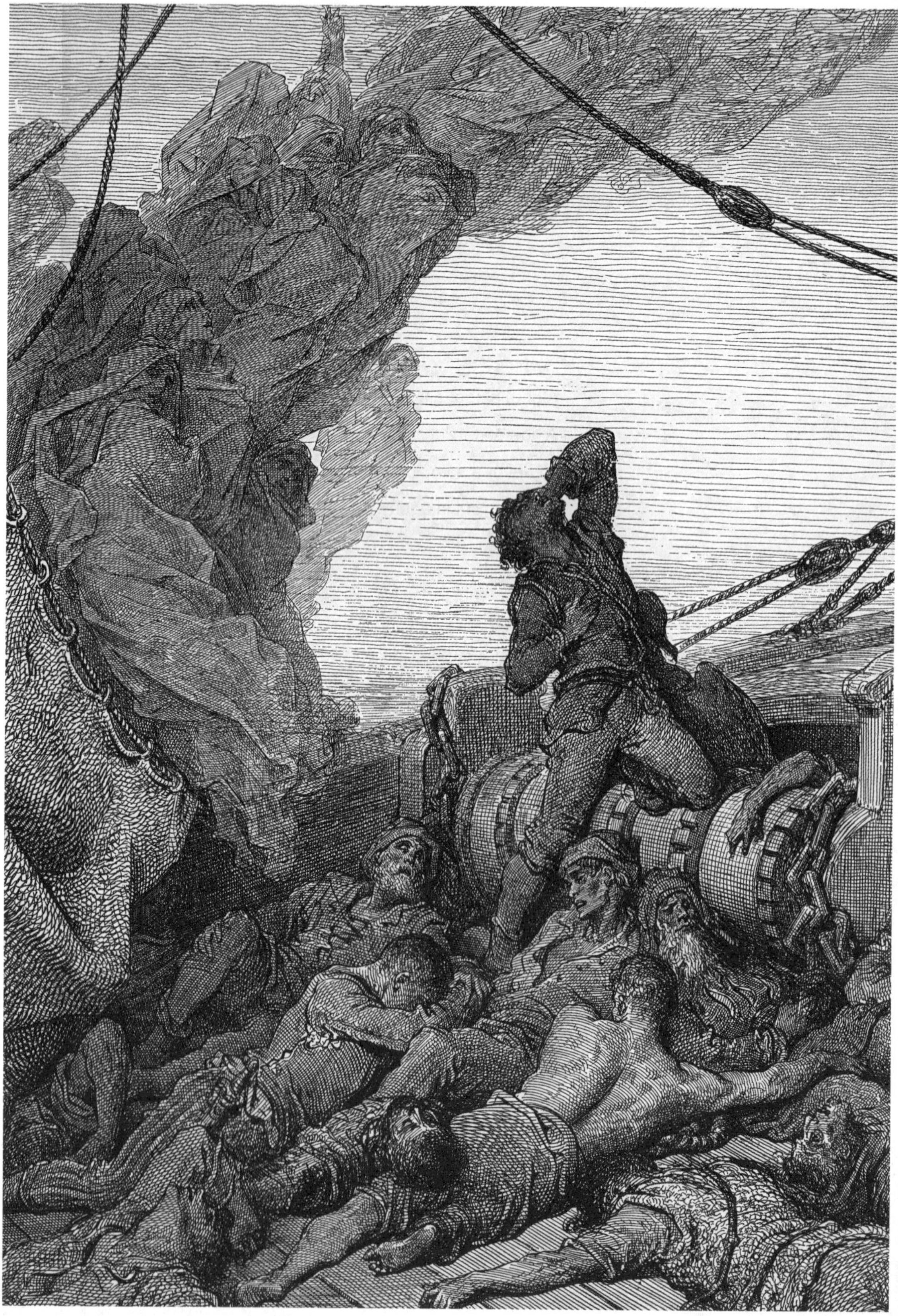

The many men, so beautiful!
And they all dead did lie:
And a thousand thousand slimy things
Lived on; and so did I.

那么多人，如此佳好！
他们皆一一身亡，
偏留下些污湿虫豸
活着；我亦未遭戕。

He despiseth the creatures of the calm,
他鄙视这些平静的生物，

I looked upon the rotting sea,
And drew my eyes away;
I looked upon the rotting deck,
And there the dead men lay.

我瞧瞧那烂的大海,
不由得双目避开;
我转身视烂的甲板,
尸首又杂乱堆排。

And envieth that they should live, and so many lie dead.
继而生出嫉妒,他们本应该活着的,却都死了。

I looked to Heaven, and tried to pray;
But or ever a prayer had gusht,
A wicked whisper came, and made
My heart as dry as dust.

仰对青天，我想祈祷；
但不待祈语出声，
即有魔语侵入双耳，
冰结了我的热诚。

I closed my lids, and kept them close,
And the balls like pulses beat;
For the sky and the sea, and the sea and the sky
Lay like a load on my weary eye,
And the dead were at my feet.

我将双目紧紧封闭，
脉搏般跳荡眼珠，
水色天光压在脸上，
令心神窘迫不舒。

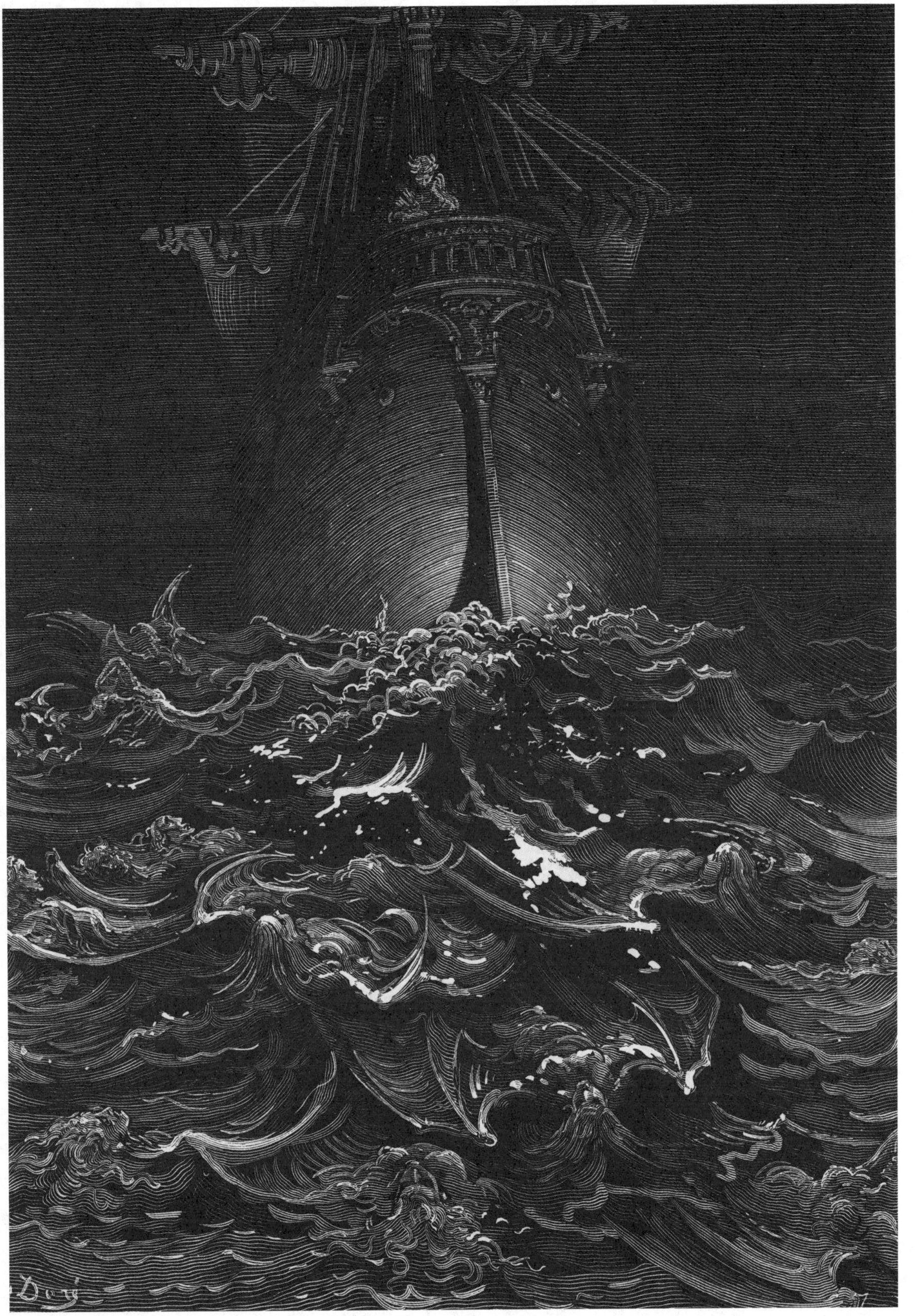

The cold sweat melted from their limbs,
Nor rot nor reek did they:
The look with which they looked on me
Had never passed away.

既无腥气，也不霉烂：
虽冷汗布满四肢，
他们眼内充满诅咒，
望着我一似生时。

But the curse liveth for him in the eye of the dead men.
死者的眼神充满了对他的诅咒。

An orphan's curse would drag to Hell
A spirit from on high;
But oh! more horrible than that
Is the curse in a dead man's eye!
Seven days, seven nights, I saw that curse,
And yet I could not die.

孤儿可以咒死神道,
更恶是死人眼睛。
它们望我七天七夜,
我想死却又不能!

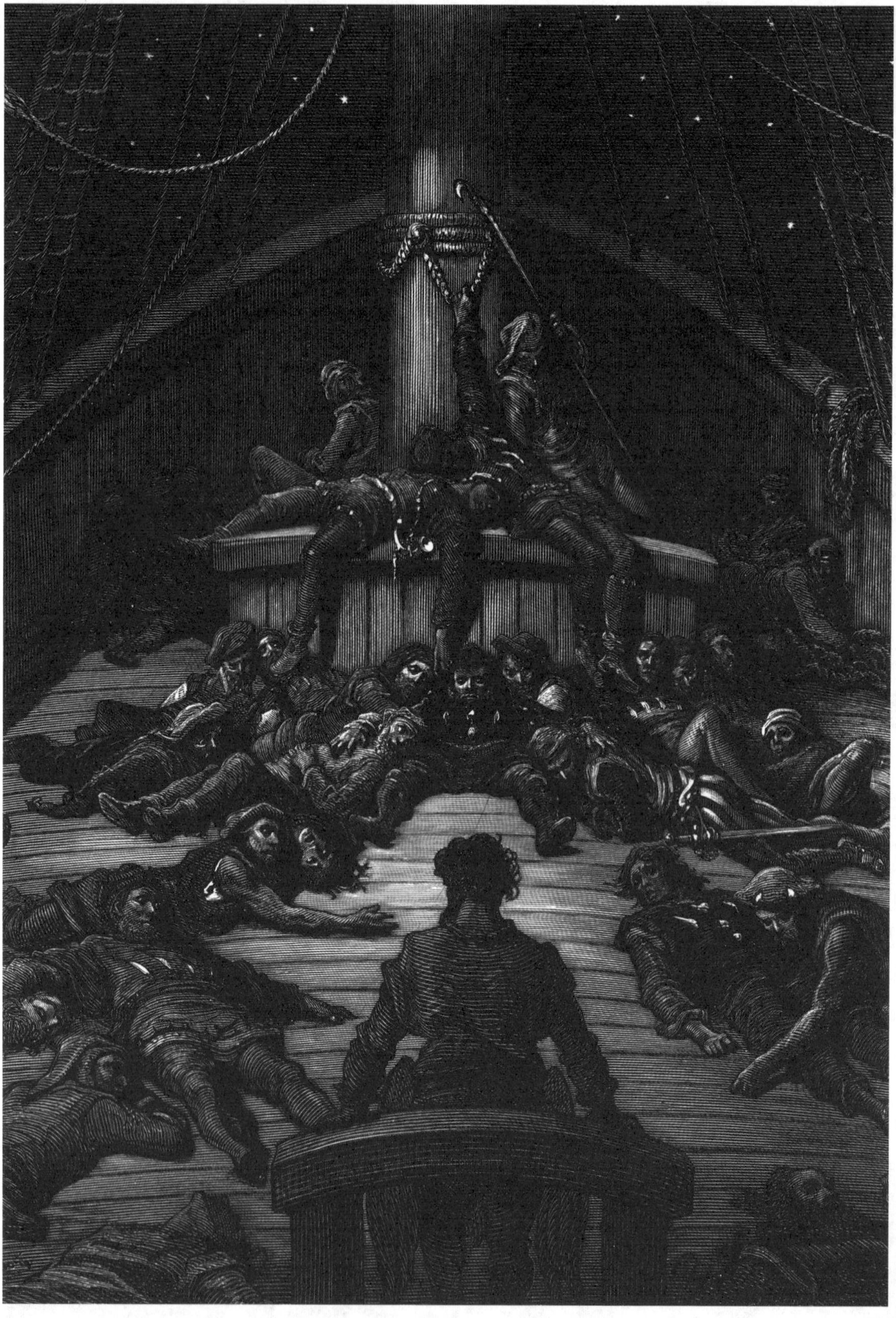

The moving Moon went up the sky,
And no where did abide:
Softly she was going up,
And a star or two beside—

我见明月自东升上，
空中行没有停留，
后边随着两三星宿，
羡妒心猛刺胸头。

In his loneliness and fixedness he yearneth towards the journeying Moon, and the stars that still sojourn, yet still move onward; and every where the blue sky belongs to them, and is their appointed rest, and their native country and their own natural homes, which they enter unannounced, as lords that are certainly expected and yet there is a silent joy at their arrival.

寂寞和不屈中，他渴望着奔向月亮的旅程，星星们有时短暂逗留，但仍伴着月亮一道行走。蓝天属于它们，似乎与它们约定了一样静止，是它们原本的国度和自己的家乡，那些叫不上名字的地方，像上帝那样确定的外部的世界，带着一丝默然的欢愉期待它们的到来。

Her beams bemocked the sultry main,
　　Like April hoar-frost spread;
But where the ship's huge shadow lay,
　　The charmed water burnt alway
　　A still and awful red.

　　她的凉光有如霜雪，
　　　　轻洒遍一片波澜；
　　但在船的巨阴之内，
　　　　水炽着深绛浓丹。

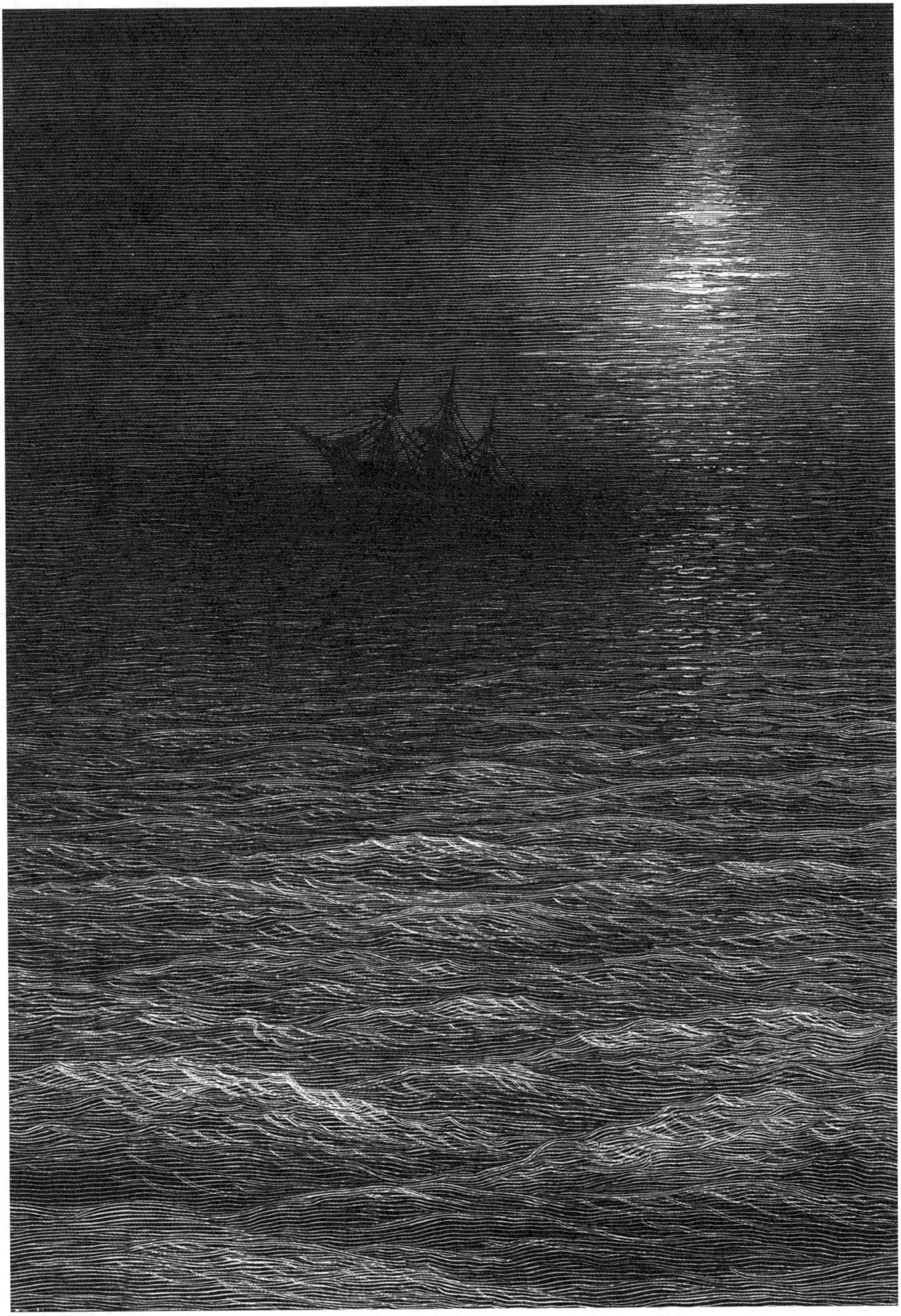

Beyond the shadow of the ship,
I watched the water-snakes:
They moved in tracks of shining white,
And when they reared, the elfish light
Fell off in hoary flakes.

水蛇游泳船阴之外：
经过处划着白痕，
它们有时掉尾而逝，
如月光射上水晶。

By the light of the Moon he beholdeth God's creatures of the great calm.
在月光下，他被笼罩在上帝的安宁中。

Within the shadow of the ship
I watched their rich attire:
Blue, glossy green, and velvet black,
They coiled and swam; and every track
Was a flash of golden fire.

水蛇游入船阴之内：
蔚蓝时色拟穹苍，
黑如深夜，绿似磷火，
经过处火赤，金黄。

O happy living things! no tongue
Their beauty might declare:
A spring of love gushed from my heart,
And I blessed them unaware:
Sure my kind saint took pity on me,
And I blessed them unaware.

热爱自我内心流出,
我双手合十胸前:
受天福呀,无忧之物!
我这般默祷上天。

Their beauty and their happiness.
He blesseth them in his heart.
他们的美丽和他们的幸福。
他在内心为他们祝福。

The self-same moment I could pray;
And from my neck so free
The Albatross fell off, and sank
Like lead into the sea."

上天对我亦加怜宥,
因海燕自我当胸,
并未待人伸手去摘,
自己便沉入海中。"

The spell begins to break.
诅咒开始破解。

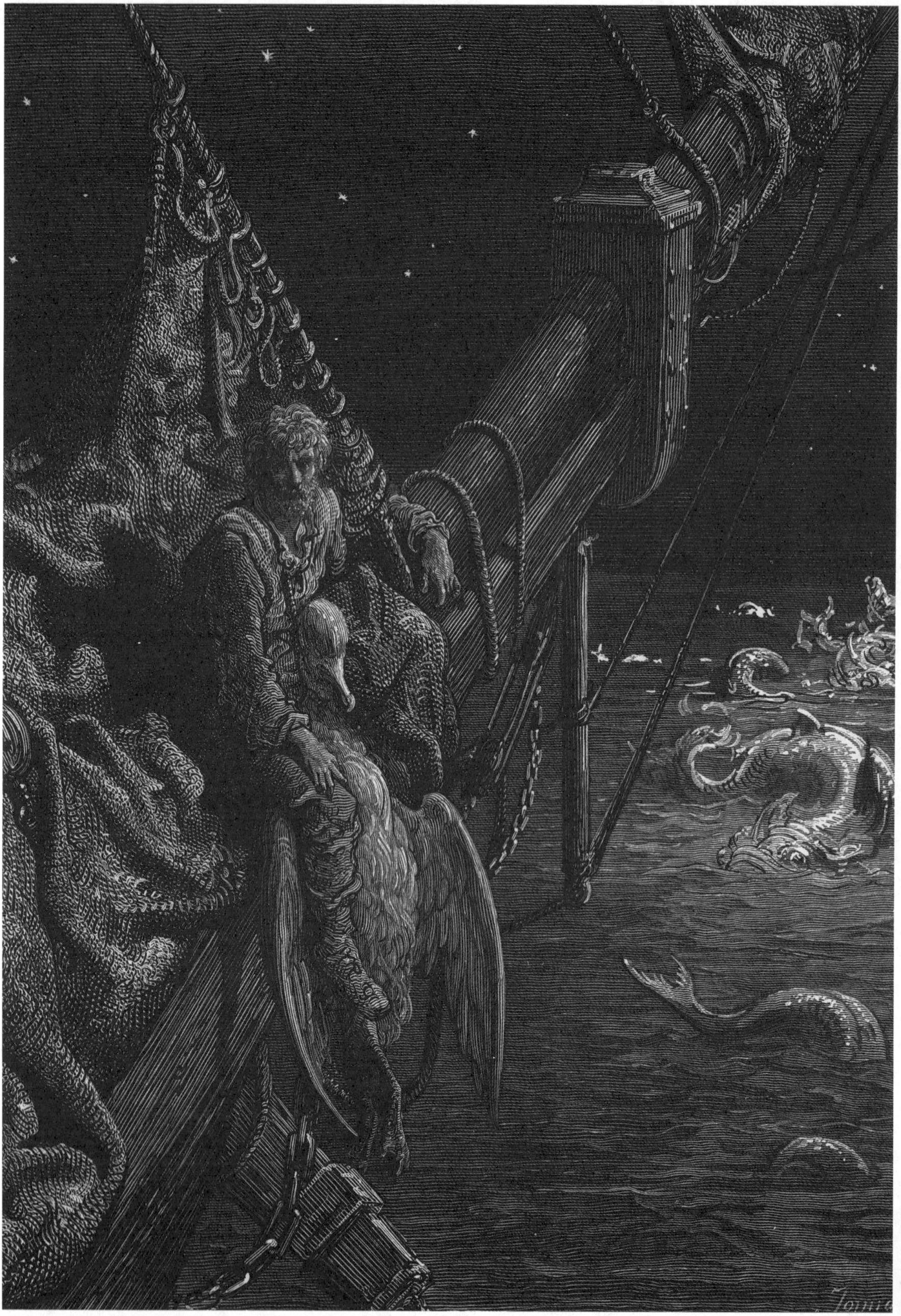

Part Five
第五部分

"OH sleep! it is a gentle thing,
Beloved from pole to pole!
To Mary Queen the praise be given!
She sent the gentle sleep from Heaven,
That slid into my soul.

"睡眠真是天之厚赐,
它可以起死回生!
它带来了甜的疲倦,
关闭起我的双睛。

The silly buckets on the deck,
That had so long remained,
I dreamt that they were filled with dew;
And when I awoke, it rained.

梦中我见船上水桶，
有甘露充满中间；
我醒转时知在下雨，
精神上顿觉新鲜。

By grace of the Holy Mother, the ancient Mariner is refreshed with rain.
在圣母的赐福下，老舟子从雨中苏醒。

My lips were wet, my throat was cold,
My garments all were dank;
Sure I had drunken in my dreams,
And still my body drank.

双唇润滑如饮仙露,
心胸上爽适清凉;
衣裳受雨将身紧贴,
如炎夏凫戏池塘。

I moved, and could not feel my limbs:
I was so light—almost
I thought that I had died in sleep,
And was a blessed ghost.

我行动时如踏云雾，
四肢与落叶同轻——
好似梦中已经死去，
如今是一个游魂。

And soon I heard a roaring wind:
It did not come anear;
But with its sound it shook the sails,
That were so thin and sere.

风飙忽在上天吼怒：
并不曾吹到此舟,
薄如纸的萎黄帆布
已作声似鬼啾啾。

He heareth sounds and seeth strange sights and commotions in the sky and the element.
他听到声响并看到一股强光在空中突然闪现，高空中突然热闹非凡。

The upper air burst into life!
And a hundred fire-flags sheen,
To and fro they were hurried about!
And to and fro, and in and out,
The wan stars danced between.

海水澄平一如明镜!
但云间闪电奔忙!
当中杂着星辰惨白,
跳跃如萤火飞扬。

And the coming wind did roar more loud,
And the sails did sigh like sedge;
And the rain poured down from one black cloud;
The Moon was at its edge.

风飙愈近呼吼愈响，
布帆作飒索芦声；
乌云之内倾下大雨；
月亮便衔着乌云。

The thick black cloud was cleft, and still
The Moon was at its side:
Like waters shot from some high crag,
The lightning fell with never a jag,
A river steep and wide.

有如岸间冲下瀑布,
闪电光直落天空——
照见乌云团团密布,
后方似达到无穷。

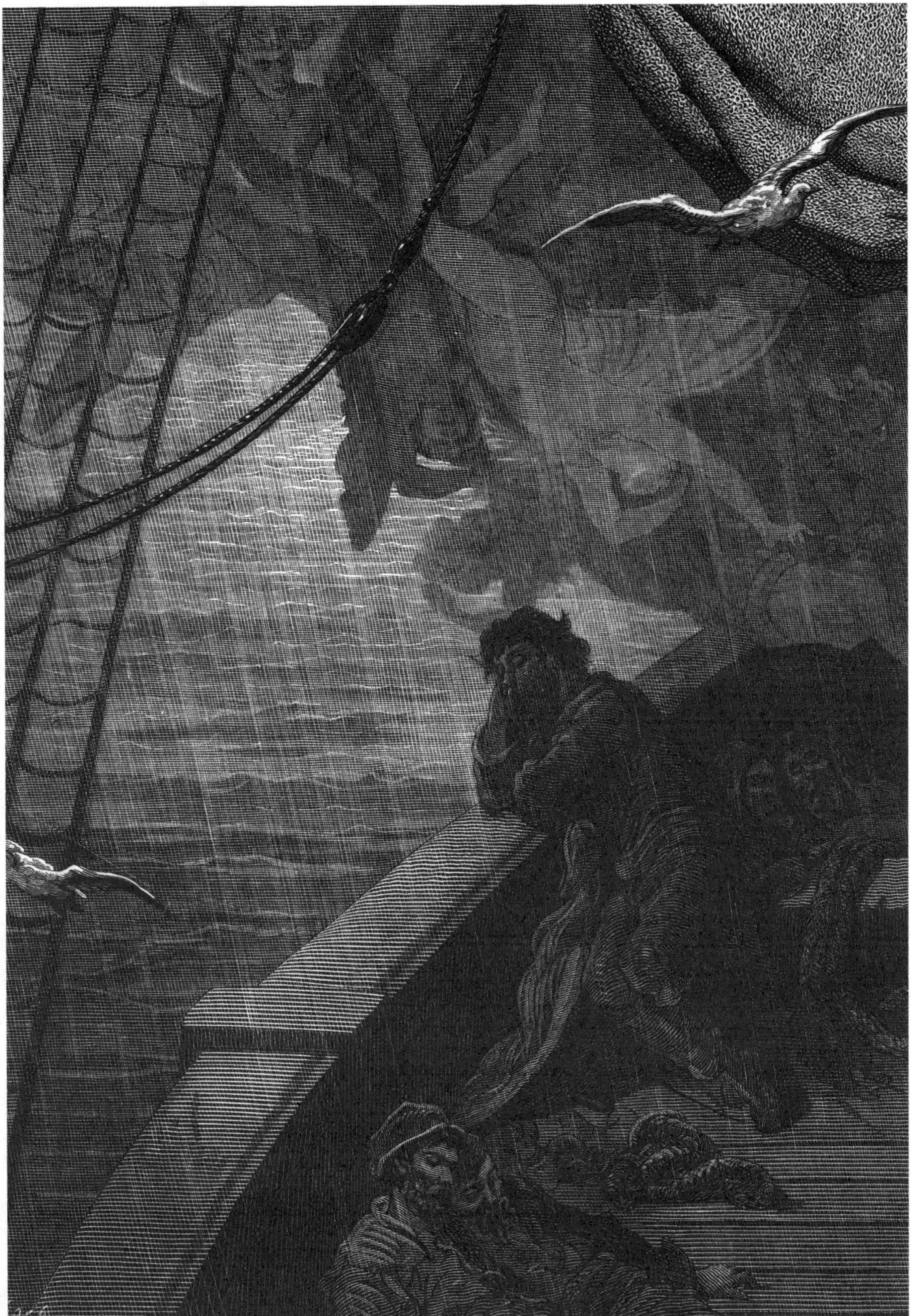

The loud wind never reached the ship,
Yet now the ship moved on!
Beneath the lightning and the Moon
The dead men gave a groan.

狂风并未吹到船上，
它自己航过洪流！
月亮紫电照见尸体，
一阵哼齐立船头。

The bodies of the ship's crew are inspired, and the ship moves on;
船员们的尸体被激发了活力，船开始移动。

They groaned, they stirred, they all uprose,
Nor spake, nor moved their eyes;
It had been strange, even in a dream,
To have seen those dead men rise.

他们默然未交一语，
木着眼不稍转移；
不说我是亲眼看见，
即梦中都要惊奇。

"The helmsman steered, the ship moved on;
Yet never a breeze up blew!
The mariners all'gan work the ropes,
Where they were wont to do:
They raised their limbs like lifeless tools—
We were a ghastly crew.

舵工把住，船舶前进；
并无风鼓起高帆！
舟子大家操纵缆索，
熟练与平日一般。

The body of my brother's son
Stood by me, knee to knee:
The body and I pulled at one rope,
But he said nought to me."

我侄儿的尸首与我
膝盖同膝盖相挨：
两人共挽一条绳索，
但他口未曾稍开。"

"I fear thee, ancient Mariner!"
"Be calm, thou Wedding-Guest!
'Twas not those souls that fled in pain,
Which to their corses came again,
But a troop of spirits blest:

"我怕你呀,老年舟子!"
"莫怕呀,赴宴嘉宾,
并非怨鬼进了躯壳,
是仙人借尸显灵。

But not by the souls of the men, nor by demons of earth or middle air, but by a blessed troop of angelic spirits, sent down by the invocation of the guardian saint.
不是因为人的灵魂,也不是因为人间或空中的精灵,而是由于一群被守护圣徒召唤而来的恩赐的仙灵,尸体被唤醒。

For when it dawned—they dropped their arms,
And clustered round the mast;
Sweet sounds rose slowly through their mouths,
And from their bodies passed.

天曙时候——他们歇手，
走向前抓住高樯，
他们口内吐出仙乐，
一声声宛转悠扬。

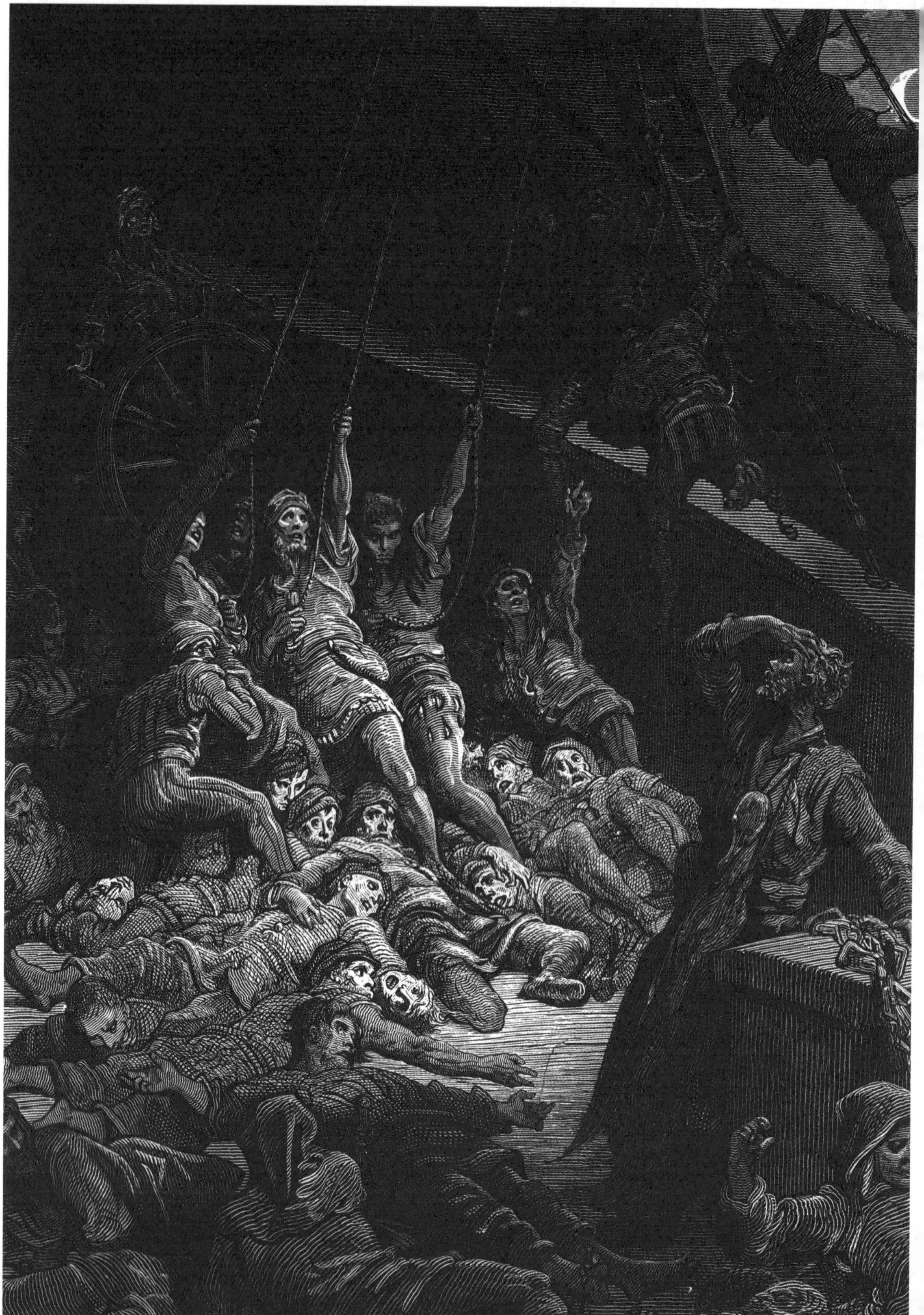

Around, around, flew each sweet sound,
Then darted to the Sun;
Slowly the sounds came back again,
Now mixed, now one by one.

时前时后，时左时右，
刹那间飞上青天；
又舒缓地降下洋面，
或同奏，或歌一仙。

Sometimes a-dropping from the sky
I heard the sky-lark sing;
Sometimes all little birds that are,
How they seemed to fill the sea and air
With their sweet jargoning!

有如云雀高歌天上，
歌声落，随了陨星；
又如林内一群小鸟
舞春风嘈杂和鸣！

And now 'twas like all instruments,
Now like a lonely flute;
And now it is an angel's song,
That makes the heavens be mute.

有如堂上管弦竞奏，
又如短笛在孤吹；
九天之内悄然谛听，
听乐神吟咏低回。

It ceased; yet still the sails made on
A pleasant noise till noon,
A noise like of a hidden brook
In the leafy month of June,
That to the sleeping woods all night
Singeth a quiet tune.

仙乐停了；帆声继作，
如初夏叶隐溪流，
午夜时向酣眠林木
低吟着歌调清幽。

Till noon we quietly sailed on,
Yet never a breeze did breathe:
Slowly and smoothly went the ship,
Moved onward from beneath.

舟安然在洋上驶过,
鼓高帆并没和风:
推舟的是南极神道,
他潜伏波浪之中。

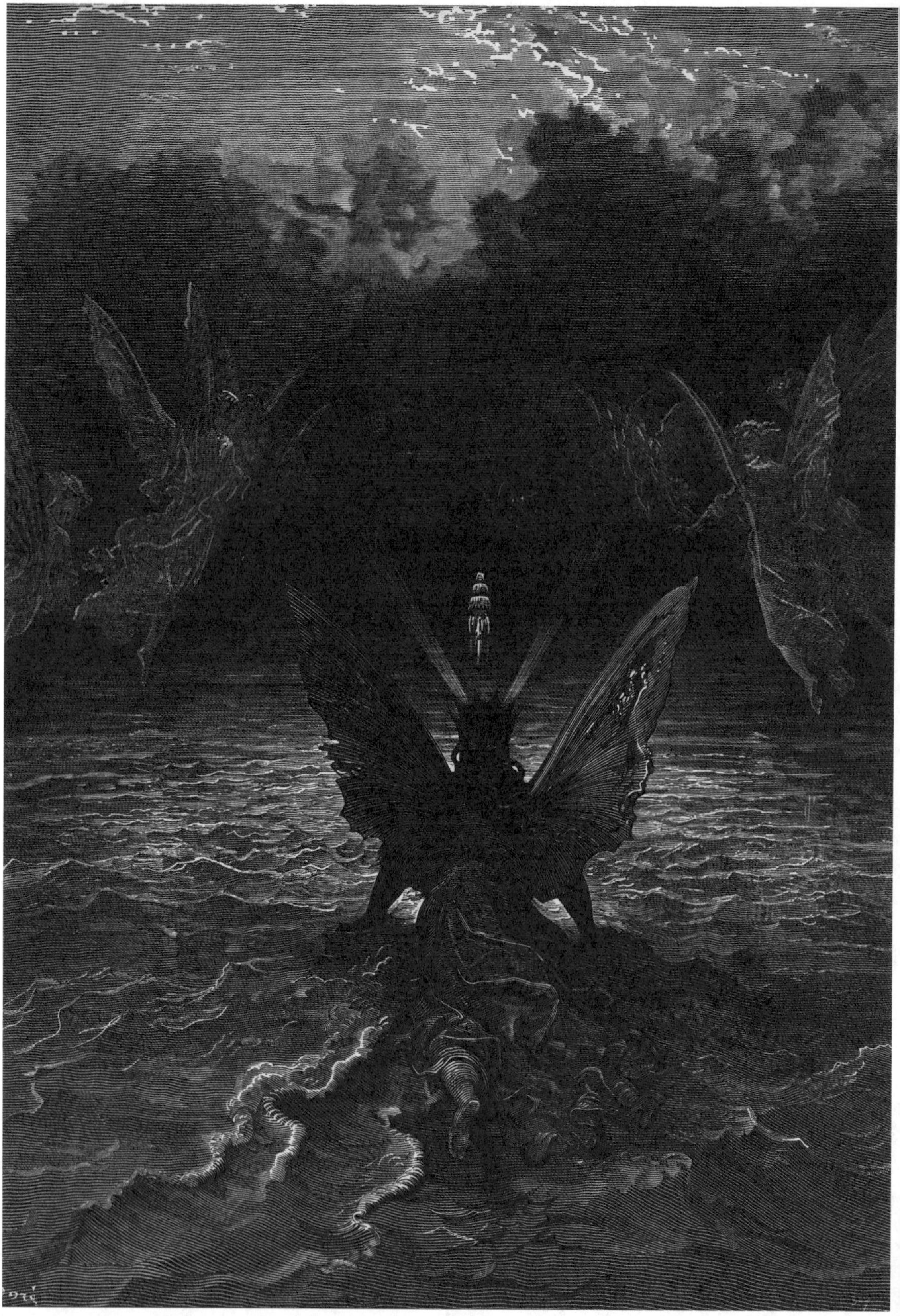

Under the keel nine fathom deep,
From the land of mist and snow,
The Spirit slid: and it was he
That made the ship to go.
The sails at noon left off their tune,
And the ship stood still also.

The Sun, right up above the mast,
Had fixed her to the ocean:
But in a minute she 'gan stir,
With a short uneasy motion—
Backwards and forwards half her length,
With a short uneasy motion.

交午时太阳在樯上
将我舟半路阻停——
隔不多时，忽前忽后，
激海水似欲重行。

The lonesome Spirit from the south-pole carries on the ship as far as the line, in obedience to the angelic troop, but still requireth vengeance.
南极神道把船带到尽可能远的海平线，虽然顺从了天使军团，但依然不忘复仇。

Then like a pawing horse let go,
She made a sudden bound:
It flung the blood into my head,
And I fell down in a swound.

有如战马喷气刨土,
缰松时一跃面前,
我舟激得通体震荡。
我晕厥身倒樯边。

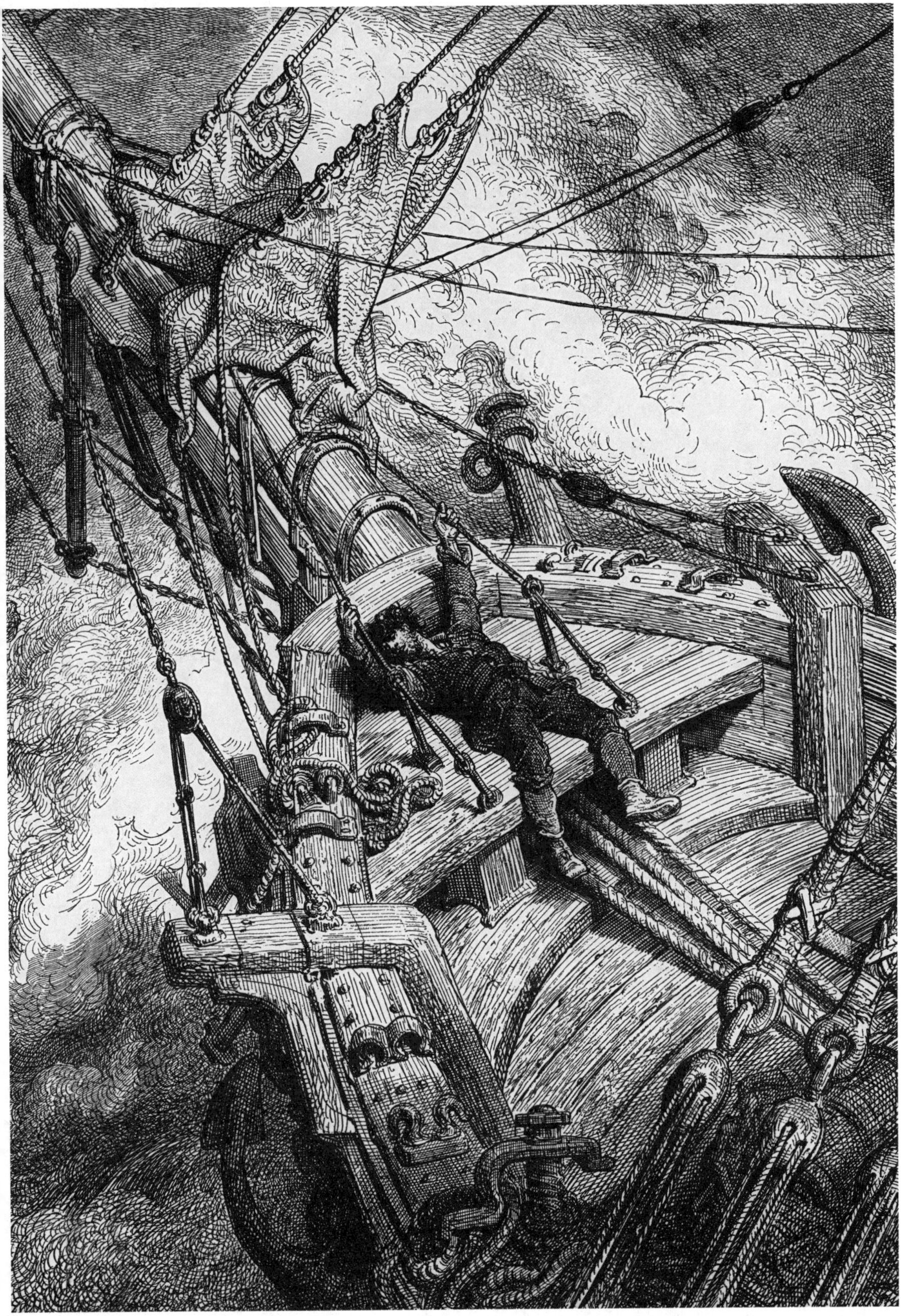

How long in that same fit I lay,

I have not to declare;

But ere my living life returned,

I heard, and in my soul discerned

Two voices in the air.

我不知道晕去多久，

但我在清醒时光，

闻见二仙在天空上

将我的罪孽评章。

'Is it he?' quoth one, 'Is this the man?
By Him who died on cross,
With his cruel bow he laid full low
The harmless Albatross.

一神仙说：'这人就是？
就是他无故伤生？
海燕于他并无妨害——
想必他残忍性成。

The spirit who bideth by himself
In the land of mist and snow,
He loved the bird that loved the man
Who shot him with his bow.'

南极神道爱此海燕,
惩残暴也是应该。
他既不知怜惜生物,
能望神恻隐为怀？'

The Polar Spirit's fellow-demons, the invisible inhabitants of the element, take part in his wrong; and two of them relate, one to the other, that penance long and heavy for the ancient Mariner hath been accorded to the Polar Spirit, who returneth southward.

南极神道的伙伴，隐形的灵魂，参与了老舟子所犯的错误。他们中的两个沆瀣一气，已将从返回南方的地极精灵而得的苦大深仇投向老舟子。

The other was a softer voice,
As soft as honey-dew:
Quoth he, 'The man hath penance done,
And penance more will do.'"

那个说时声调和缓，
轻如露落下虚空。
他说：'此人已经忏悔，
再忏悔便能避凶。'"

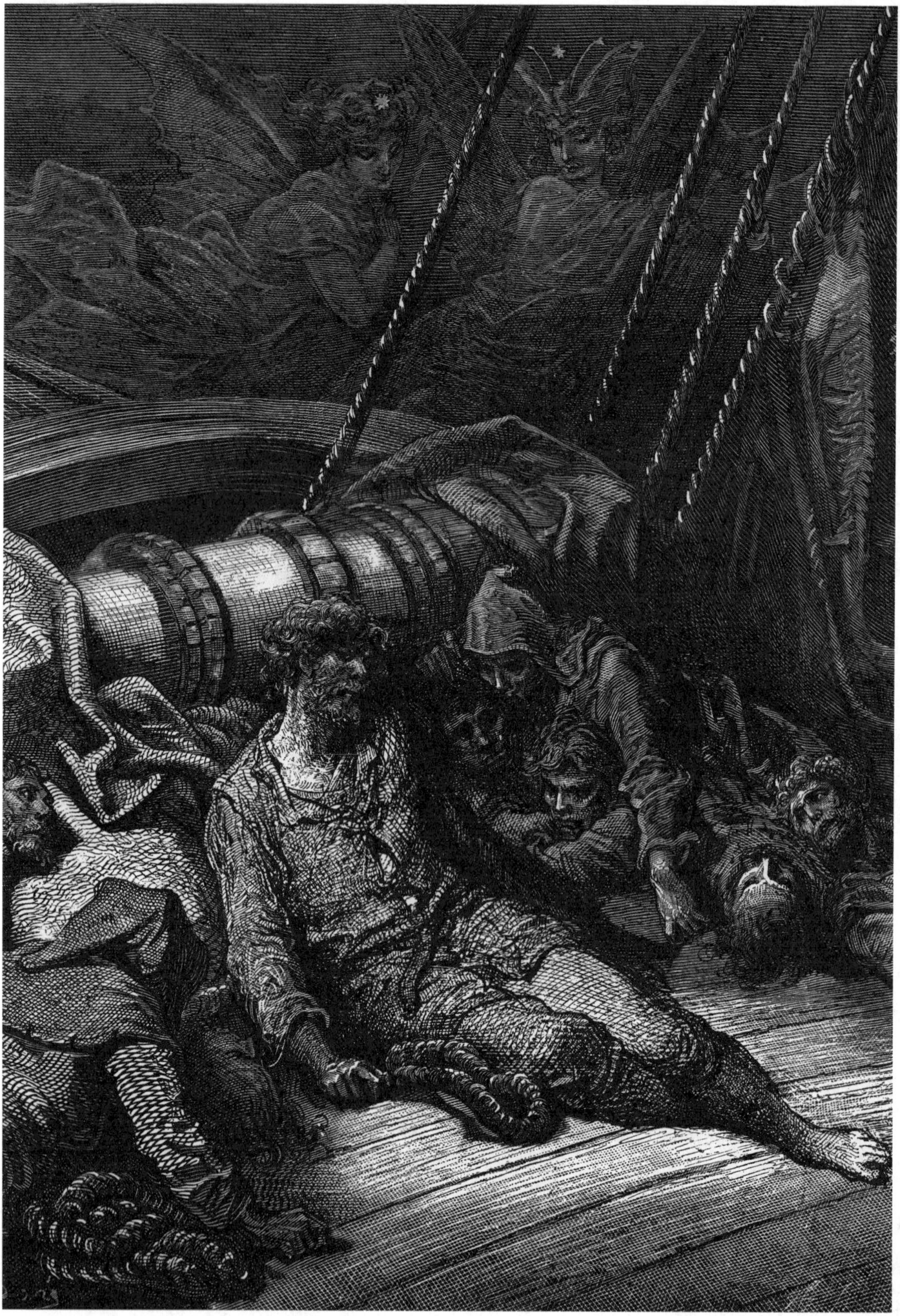

Part Six

第六部分

"FIRST VOICE：

'BUT tell me, tell me! speak again,

Thy soft response renewing—

What makes that ship drive on so fast?

What is the ocean doing?'

"第一个声音：

'有一桩事我不明白，

还望你告我得知——

船何故能行得那快，

在风乎水定之时？'

SECOND VOICE:

'Still as a slave before his lord,

The ocean hath no blast;

His great bright eye most silently

Up to the Moon is cast—

第二个声音：

'洋无风飙不能作浪，

是月亮操着大权。

他见月亮换了标志，

才有风，或起波澜——

If he may know which way to go;
For she guides him smooth or grim.
See, brother, see! how graciously
She looketh down on him.'

极神将事告知月亮,
她也说舟子残生
该受惩罚：是她命令
风飙息波浪不兴。'

FIRST VOICE:

'But why drives on that ship so fast,

Without or wave or wind?'

SECOND VOICE:

'The air is cut away before,

And closes from behind.

'幸有天仙为他缓颊,
说教他痛悔前非。'
'神允了,推舟到赤道,
即要携我辈同归。[1]

The Mariner hath been cast into a trance; for the angelic power causeth the vessel to drive northward faster than human life could endure.
舟子驱船向东行驶,但是,天使让船向北航行的力量远远大过人类所能承受的。

[1] 杨德豫先生在《柯尔律治诗选》(广西师范大学出版社,2009年4月第一版)中将本段译作:"第一个声音:'海上不起浪,也不见风来,船怎么走得这么快?'第二个声音:'在船的前面,大气被劈开;后面,又合成一块。'"

Fly, brother, fly! more high, more high!
Or we shall be belated:
For slow and slow that ship will go,
When the Mariner's trance is abated.'

仙兄，飞上，再飞上点，
让我们速返南方。
舟子梦中苏醒之后，
船自能缓缓前航。'

I woke, and we were sailing on
As in a gentle weather:
'Twas night, calm night, the moon was high;
The dead men stood together.

我醒回了,见船前进,
如和风助浪推舟:
天水澄平,月光明朗;
但死尸复立船头。

The supernatural motion is retarded; the Mariner awakes, and his penance begins anew.
超自然的力量消失,老舟子苏醒了,又开始了新的忏悔。

All stood together on the deck,
For a charnel-dungeon fitter:
All fixed on me their stony eyes,
That in the Moon did glitter.

他们聚在甲板之上，
似墓中冷气森森：
他们向我瞪着鱼眼，
瞳子上反射月明。

The pang, the curse, with which they died,
Had never passed away:
I could not draw my eyes from theirs,
Nor turn them up to pray.

他们死时剧痛诅咒
到如今尚未祛消——
他们吸住我的双目，
勾起我愧悔如潮。

And now this spell was snapt; once more
I viewed the ocean green,
And looked far forth, yet little saw
Of what had else been seen—

谢天释了我的双目！
我原可瞻望流连，
但我无心眺入辽远，
因恐惧在我胸间——

The curse is finally expiated.
诅咒最终被解除了。

Like one, that on a lonesome road
Doth walk in fear and dread,
And having once turned round walks on,
And turns no more his head;
Because he knows, a frightful fiend
Doth close behind him tread.

有如深夜人过荒径，
身后似有鬼相追，
转弯时候不敢回首，
鼓起气行步如飞。

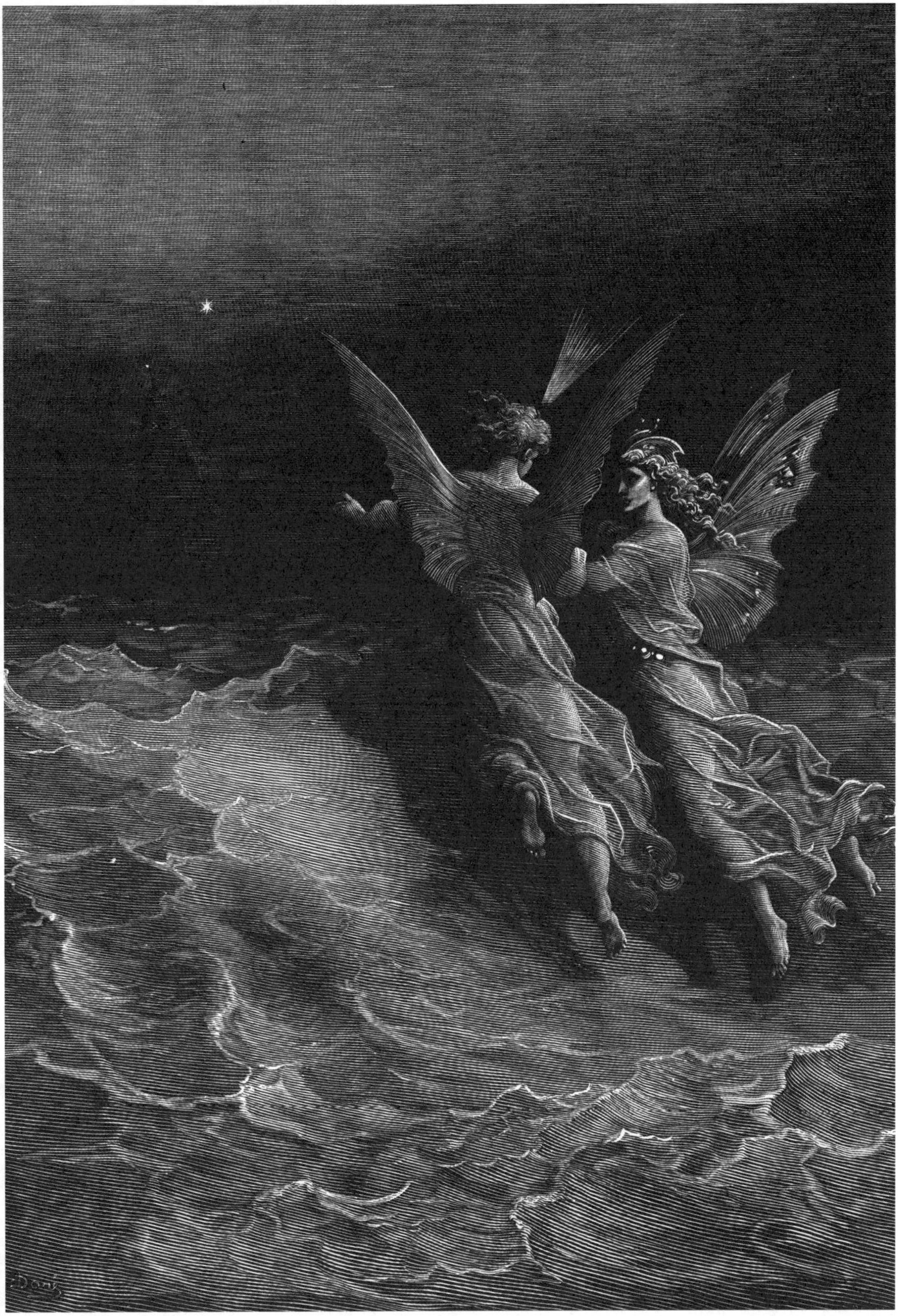
Doré

But soon there breathed a wind on me,

Nor sound nor motion made:

Its path was not upon the sea,

In ripple or in shade.

来了轻风拂我颜面,
它无声亦未兴波:
海上并无它的踪迹,
唯有我觉它抚摩。

It raised my hair, it fanned my cheek

Like a meadow-gale of spring—

It mingled strangely with my fears,

Yet it felt like a welcoming.

异风飘漾我的额发,

似春飔吹过草坪——

一方我的惊骇愈甚,

一方又引起欢欣。

Swiftly, swiftly flew the ship,
Yet she sailed softly too;
Sweetly, sweetly blew the breeze—
On me alone it blew.

飞呀,飞呀,船舶驶着,
在无风无浪之洋;
轻呀,轻呀,异风拂着,
掀起了我的衣裳。

Oh! dream of joy! is this indeed
The light-house top I see?
Is this the hill? is this the kirk?
Is this mine own countree?

前面那不就是灯塔？
这真是喜降自天！
那不就是青葱山色？
那不是教堂塔尖？

And the ancient Mariner beholdeth his native country.
老舟子返回了他的家乡。

We drifted o'er the harbour-bar,
And I with sobs did pray—
O let me be awake, my God!
Or let me sleep alway.

船只安然航进港口，
我喜极珠泪双流——
帝呀，让我心神清醒！
不然就死在船头。

The harbour-bay was clear as glass,
So smoothly it was strewn!
And on the bay the moonlight lay,
And the shadow of the Moon.

港中海水一平如镜,
倒映着山色葱茏!
波间浮起一轮明月,
又一轮悬挂天空。

The rock shone bright, the kirk no less,
That stands above the rock:
The moonlight steeped in silentness
The steady weathercock.

月光之内山岩发光，
有教堂立在崖阴：
空中不听一丝声息，
塔尖上眠了风针。

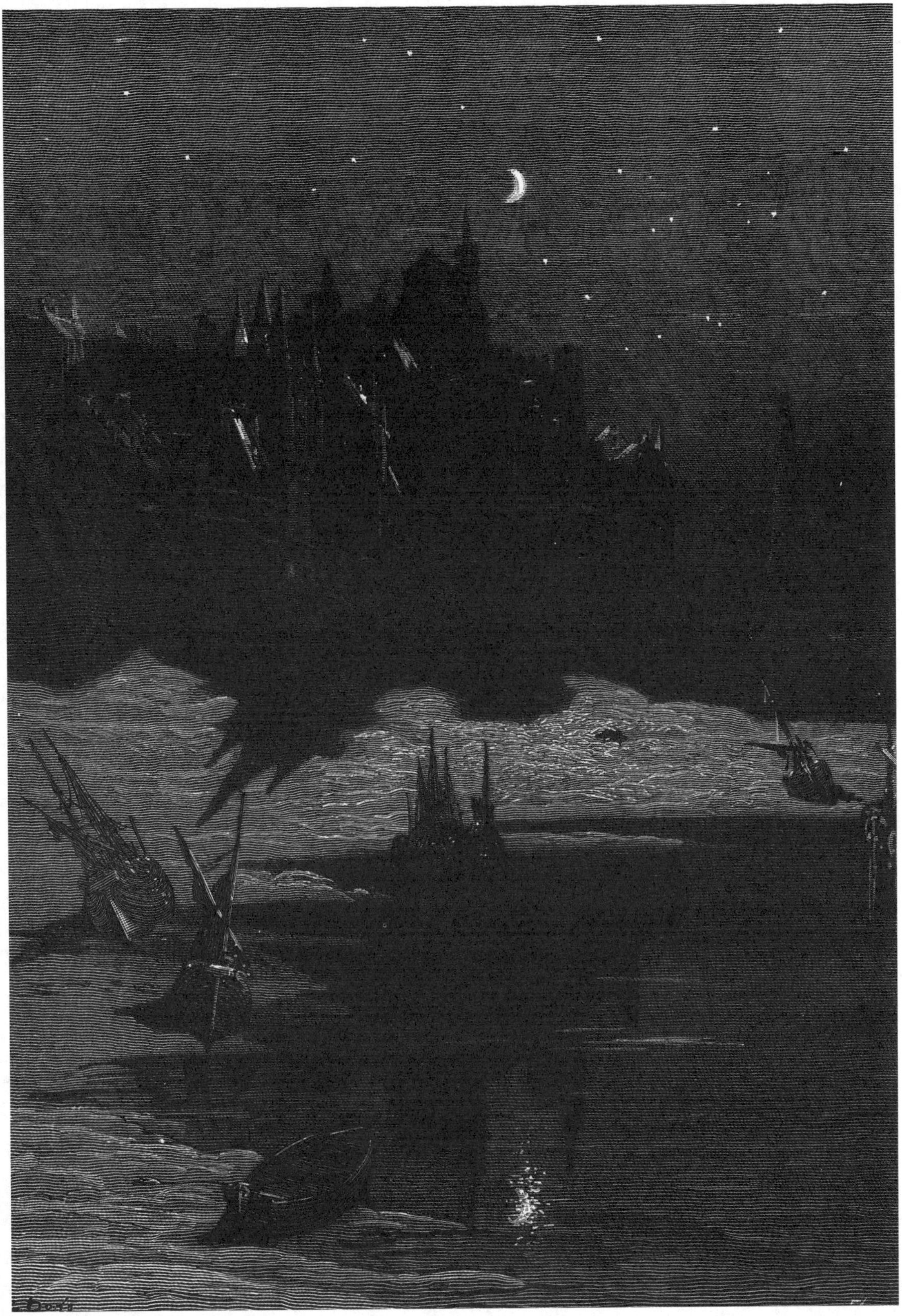

And the bay was white with silent light,

Till rising from the same,

Full many shapes, that shadows were,

In crimson colors came.

一片银色港水之上,

忽生出点点红光,

它们不像渔舟、灯塔,

都漂来我的船旁。

The angelic spirits leave the dead bodies,
仙灵们离开了死尸,

A little distance from the prow
Those crimson shadows were:
I turned my eyes upon the deck—
Oh, Christ! what saw I there!

它们是些赤色阴影，
向船头舒缓飘来。
一眨眼间再望船板——
惊得我目瞪口呆！

And appear in their own forms of light.
重现出他们本来的光辉。

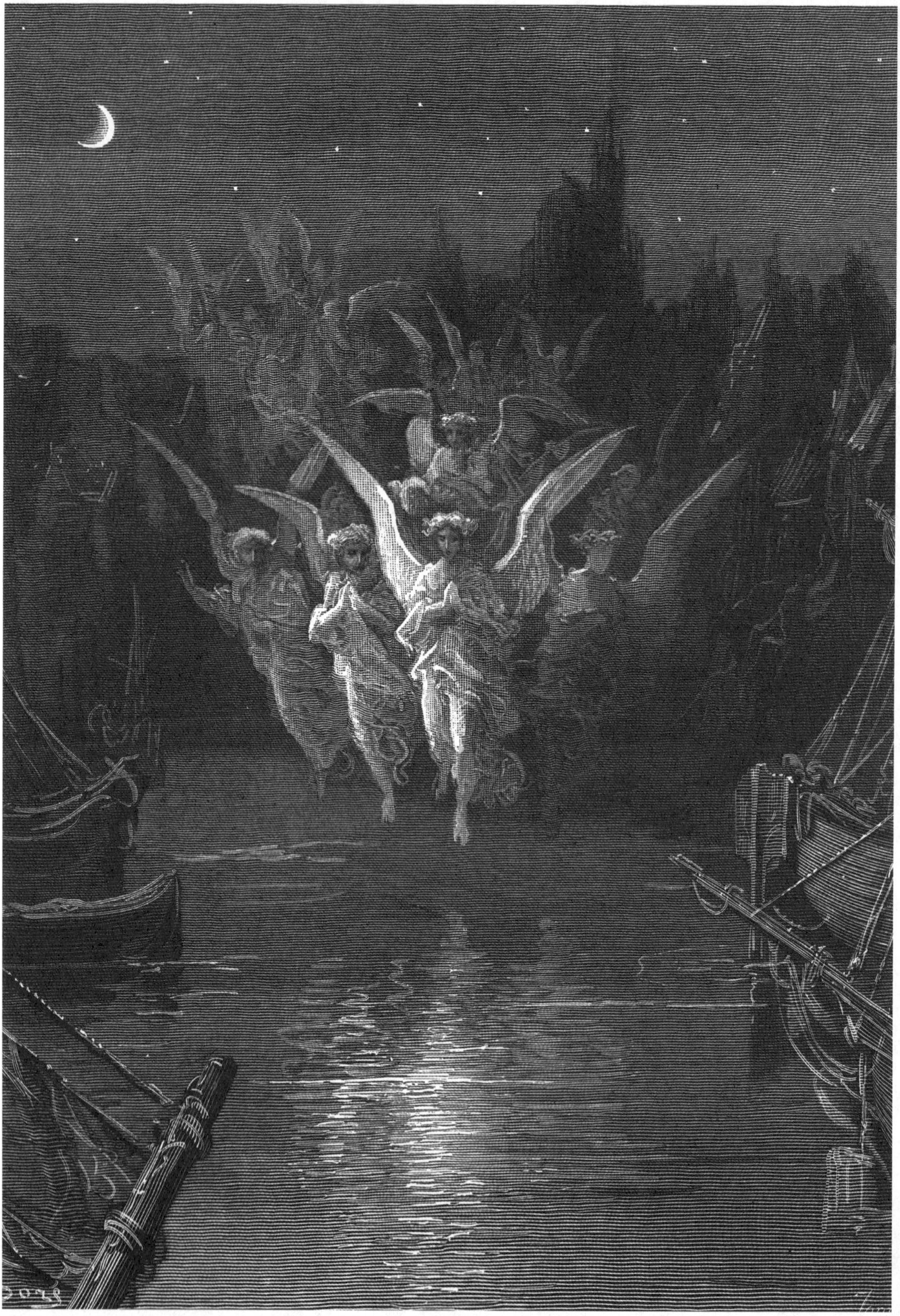

Each corse lay flat, lifeless and flat,
And, by the holy rood!
A man all light, a seraph-man,
On every corse there stood.

死尸仍旧纵横船上，
但双足跨上尸身，
便是刚才那些赤影，
他们是通体光明。

This seraph-band, each waved his hand:

It was a heavenly sight!

They stood as signals to the land,

Each one a lovely light;

这些仙人皆在挥手,

异光充满舟中。

他们像是示知岸上,

以灯光相似之红。

This seraph-band, each waved his hand,
No voice did they impart—
No voice; but oh! the silence sank
Like music on my heart.

这些仙人皆在挥手,
挥手时默无一言——
啊,这无言便如音乐,
舒畅了我的胸间。

But soon I heard the dash of oars,
I heard the Pilot's cheer;
My head was turned perforce away
And I saw a boat appear.

不久我闻桨声欸乃，
领港唤：'谁在前方？'
我将双目挪过观看，
是一船来我身旁。

The Pilot and the Pilot's boy,
I heard them coming fast:
Dear Lord in Heaven! it was a joy
The dead men could not blast.

领港人与他的儿子
划着船刻不留停。
天哪,我想,这真侥幸。
我便要离去尸身。

I saw a third—I heard his voice:
It is the Hermit good!
He singeth loud his godly hymns
That he makes in the wood.
He'll shrieve my soul, he'll wash away
The Albatross's blood."

还有一人，那是隐士，
他奉神栖宿林中。
他将涤净海鸭之血
自我的忏悔心胸。"

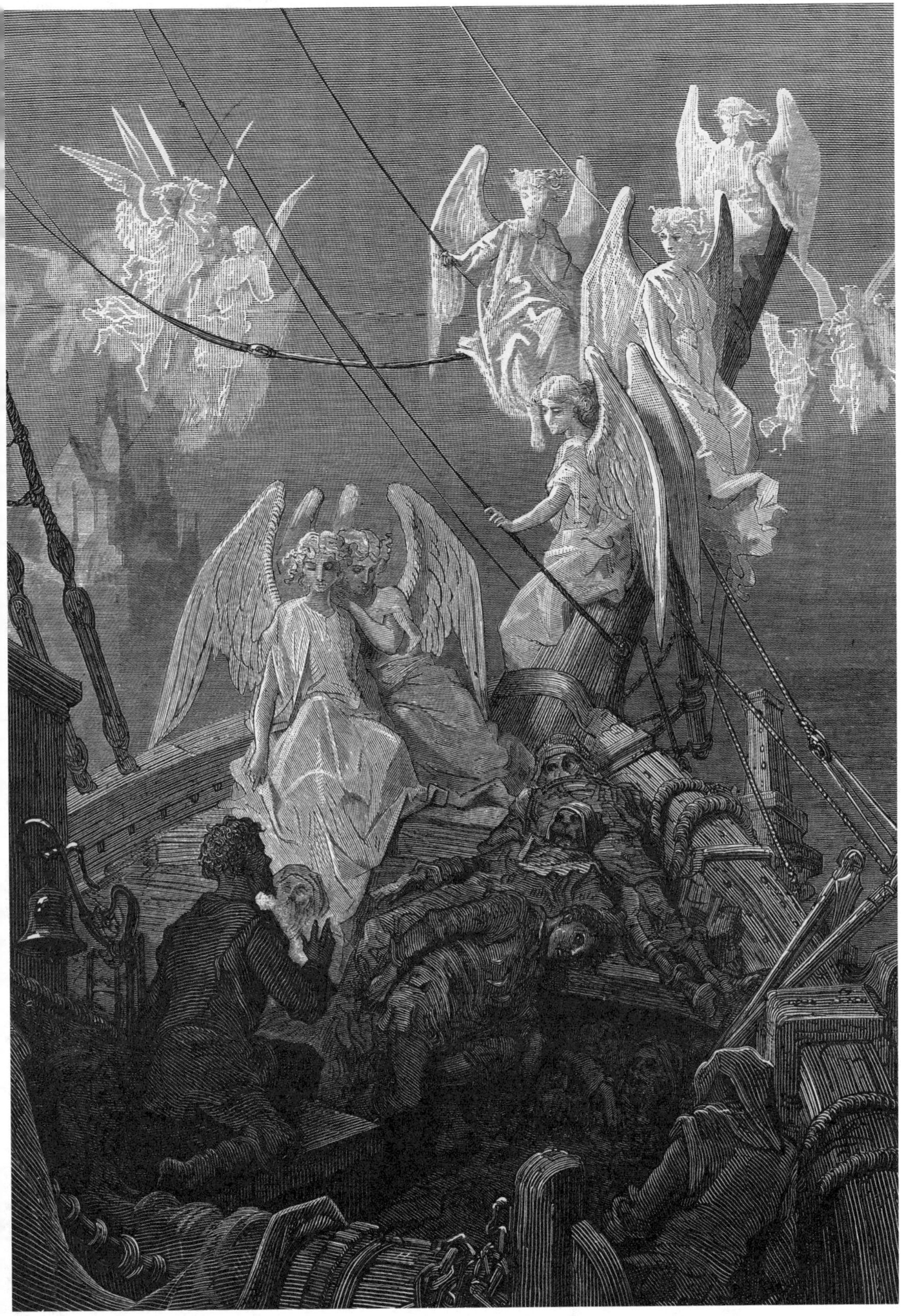

Part Seven
第七部分

"THIS Hermit good lives in that wood
　　Which slopes down to the sea.
How loudly his sweet voice he rears!
　　He loves to talk with marineres
　　That come from a far countree.

　　"他独居在海边林内。
　　　晨与昏高唱颂诗。
　　他喜问询远游舟子
　　　在船归故国之时。

The Hermit of the wood,
山林中的隐士，

He kneels at morn, and noon, and eve—
He hath a cushion plump:
It is the moss that wholly hides
The rotted old oak-stump.

他有膝垫柔如绒制，
祈祷时日用三回：
那是橡树余的根节，
苔生满上面、周围。

The skiff-boat neared: I heard them talk,
　'Why, this is strange, I trow!
Where are those lights so many and fair,
　That signal made but now?'

　　小舟近时我闻言语:
　　'这桩事真正稀奇:
　　刚才看见红光相召,
　　走来了哪知被欺!'

'Strange, by my faith!' the Hermit said—
'And they answered not our cheer!
The planks look warped! and see those sails,
How thin they are and sere!
I never saw aught like to them,
Unless perchance it were

隐士也道：'奇怪，奇怪！
我们唤不听回声！
船板裂了！那些帆布
薄如纸又显凋零：

Approacheth the ship with wonder.
在惊奇中，船靠近了。

Brown skeletons of leaves that lag
My forest-brook along;
When the ivy-tod is heavy with snow,
And the owlet whoops to the wolf below,
That eats the she-wolf's young.'

似黄叶悬树的骨架，
在藤萝复雪时光，
上头有枭怪声叫唤，
狼在下吞食小狼。'

'Dear Lord! it hath a fiendish look—
(The Pilot made reply)
I am a-feared.' — 'Push on, push on!'
Said the Hermit cheerily.

'这船看来形状不妙，
我不敢还向前划。'
领港人说。'划上前去，'
隐士拿慰语相加。

The boat came closer to the ship,
But I nor spake nor stirred;
The boat came close beneath the ship,
And straight a sound was heard.

小舟向我慢慢行近,
我无言亦未挪身。
小舟到了我的船下,
港水中忽发大声。

Under the water it rumbled on,
Still louder and more dread:
It reached the ship, it split the bay;
The ship went down like lead.

隆隆有似雷霆下降，
愈近时声响愈高。
触上船时一声爆裂，
船如铅立沉怒涛。

The ship suddenly sinketh.
船突然下沉。

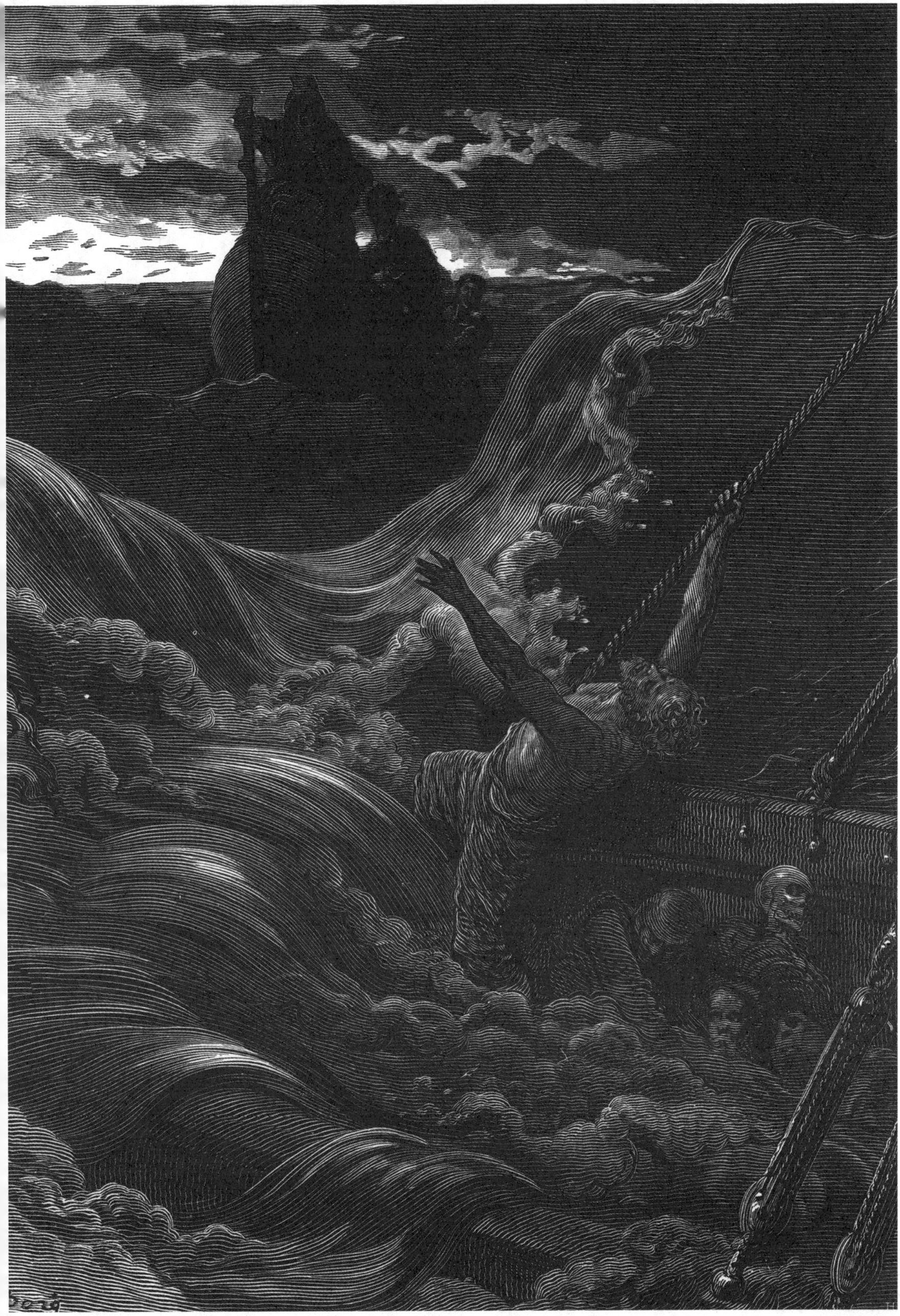

Stunned by that loud and dreadful sound,
Which sky and ocean smote,
Like one that hath been seven days drowned
My body lay afloat;
But swift as dreams, myself I found
Within the Pilot's boat.

这声炸裂惊天动海,
震得我魂飞耳聋;
等我悠悠魂魄清醒,
见已身在小舟中。

Tile ancient Mariner is saved in the Pilot's boat.
老舟子在领港人的船上得救了。

Upon the whirl, where sank the ship,

The boat spun round and round;

And all was still, save that the hill

Was telling of the sound.

那条船在旋涡之内

螺丝样沉入波澜。

波纹渐大，渐渐消灭，

剩四围回响空山。

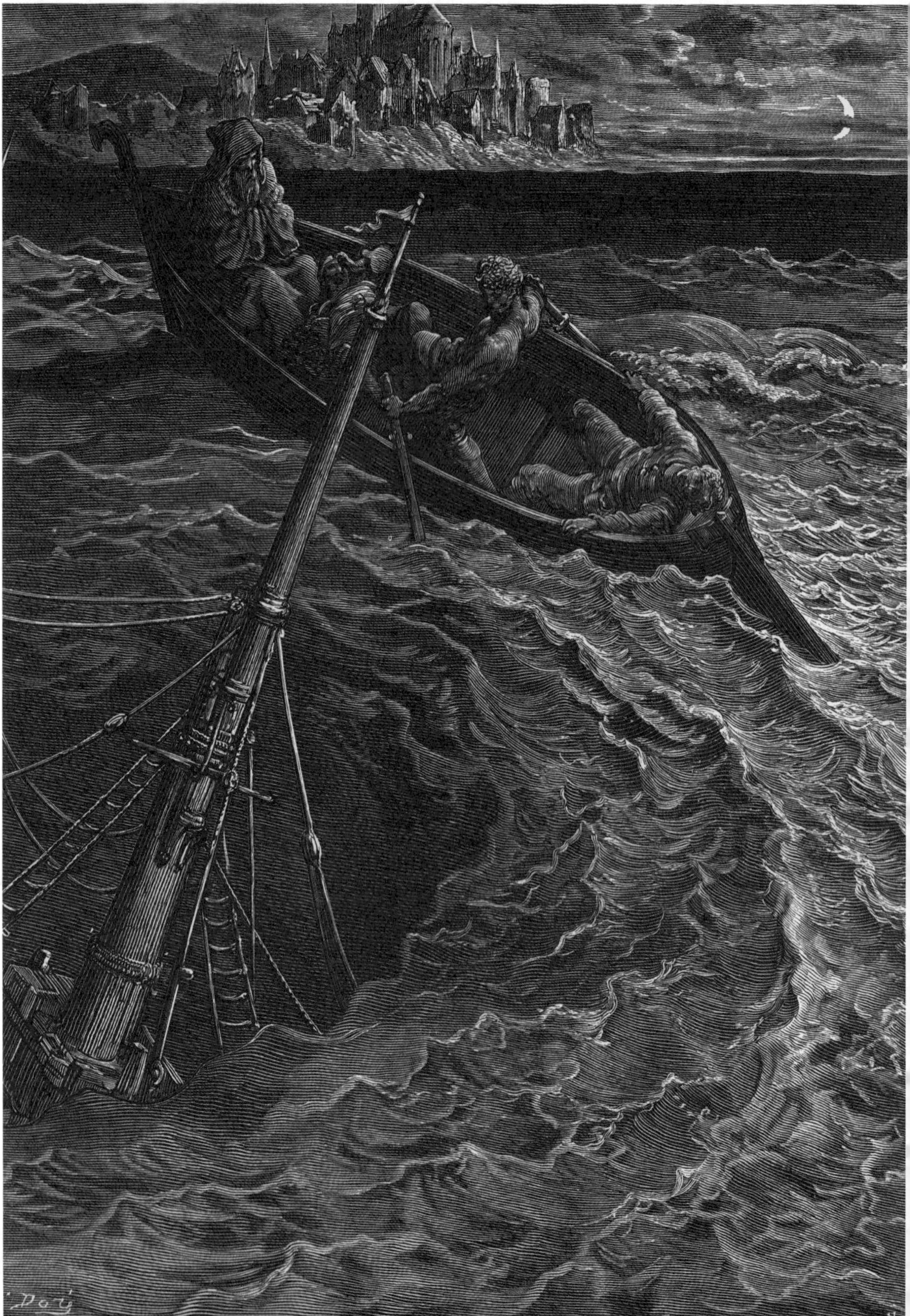

I moved my lips—the Pilot shrieked
And fell down in a fit;
The holy Hermit raised his eyes,
And prayed where he did sit.

领港人才见我开口,
一声叫便倒船头。
隐士也将双目高举,
唇动着向天默求。

I took the oars: the Pilot's boy,
Who now doth crazy go,
Laughed loud and long, and all the while
His eyes went to and fro.
'Ha! ha!' quoth he, 'full plain I see,
The Devil knows how to row.'

疯了领港人的儿子,
他见我荡桨青波,
'我知道了,哈哈!'他笑,
'鬼也会划船渡河。'

And now, all in my own countree,
I stood on the firm land!
The Hermit stepped forth from the boat,
And scarcely he could stand.

我这已经脚登实地?
我已经回了家乡?
隐士也从舟中上岸,
他软如醉汉郎当。

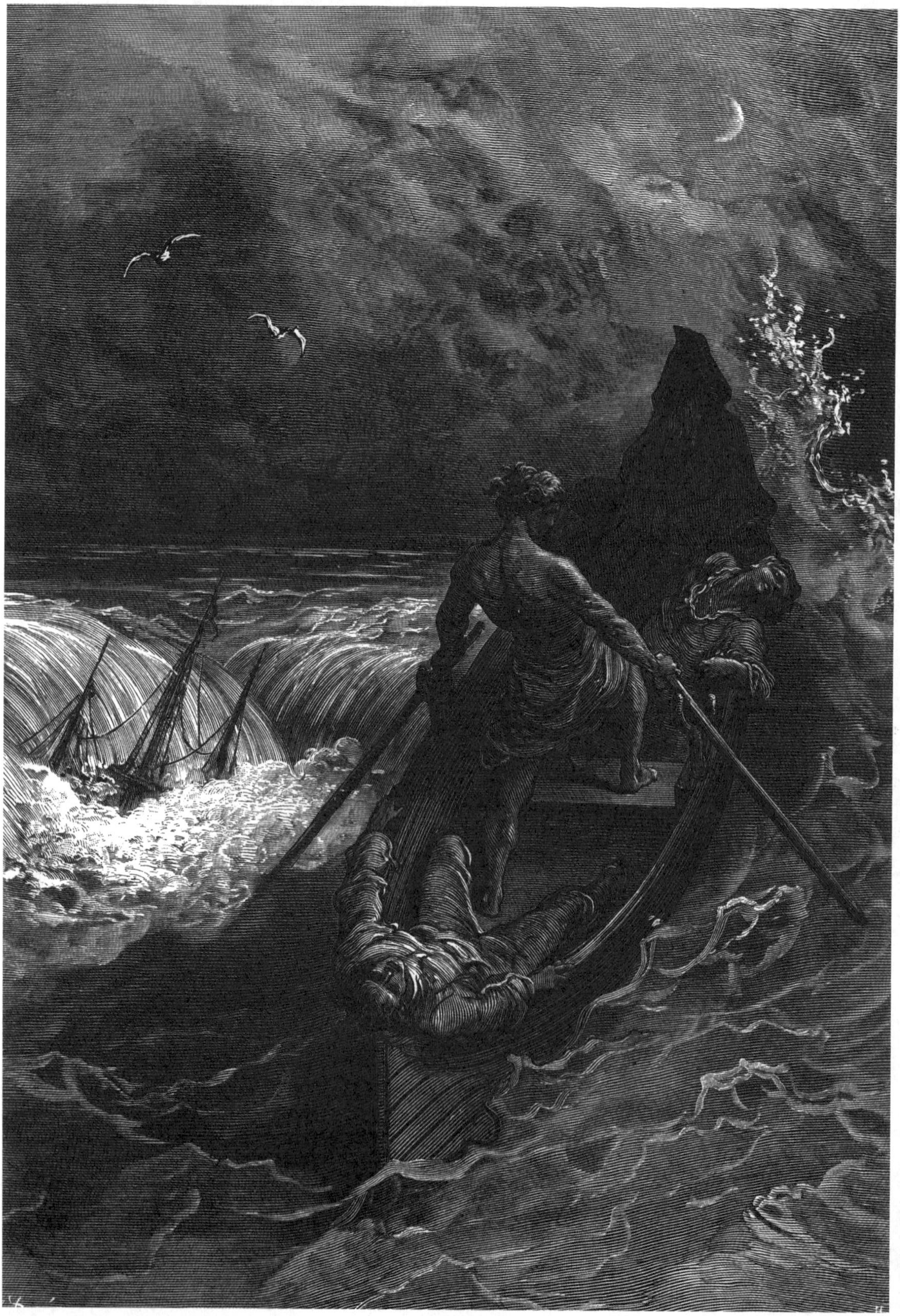

'O shrieve me, shrieve me, holy man!'
The Hermit crossed his brow.
'Say quick,' quoth he, 'I bid thee say—
What manner of man art thou?'

'救我，救我！'我求隐士。
他举手合十胸襟。
'你说，你说，'他开言道，
'你是鬼还是生人？'

The ancient Mariner earnestly entreateth the Hermit to shrieve him; and the penance of life falls on him.
老舟子诚恳地祈求隐士洗净他的罪，清除他身上沾染的忏悔。

Forthwith this frame of mine was wrenched
With a woful agony,
Which forced me to begin my tale;
And then it left me free.

我闻此语抽了一下，
如利刀割我心肝，
不得不将往事详叙；
叙毕时方觉泰然。

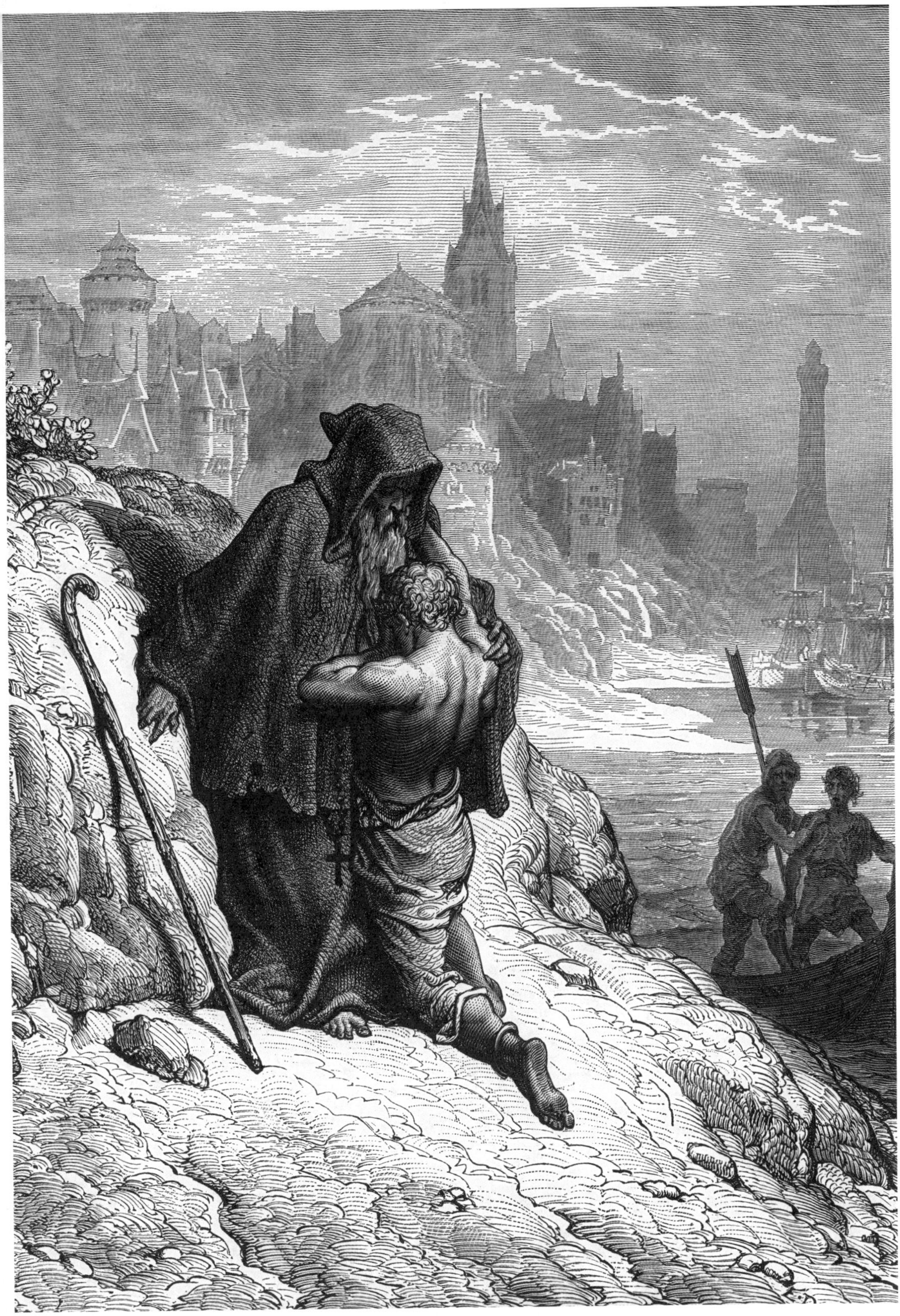

Since then, at an uncertain hour,
That agony returns:
And till my ghastly tale is told,
This heart within me burns.

此后常来一阵剧痛
盘踞在我的心头：
必要前事重述一遍，
心灵内方觉自由。

And ever and anon throughout his future life an agony constraineth him to travel from land to land.
说不准何时，未来的某一天，那痛苦又来囚禁他的时候，他不得不再次重复之前的旅程，从一个地方到另一个地方。

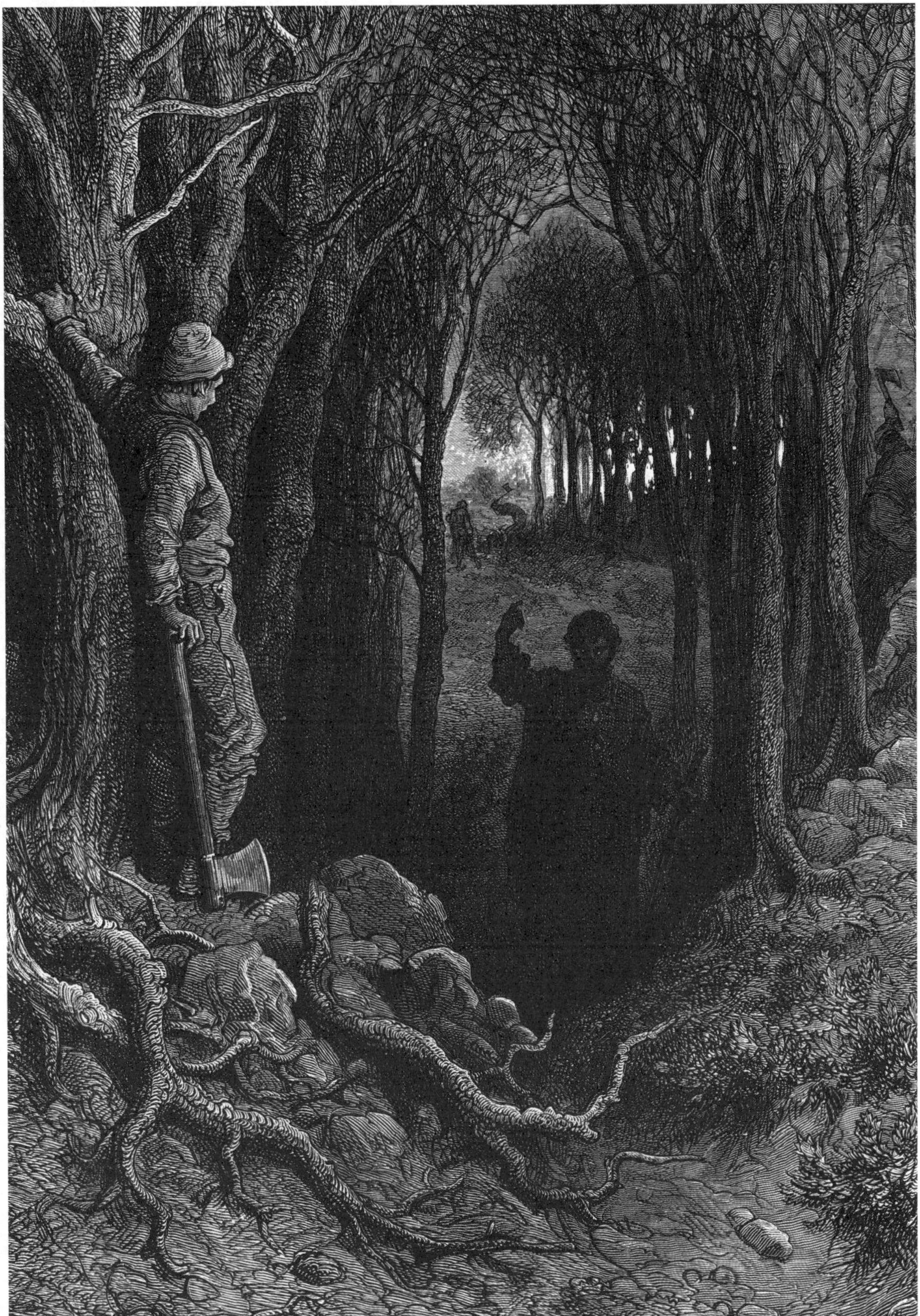

I pass, like night, from land to land;

I have strange power of speech;

That moment that his face I see,

I know the man that must hear me:

To him my tale I teach.

从此我的谈锋健利。

我如夜飘过四方。

何人应听我的故事，

我一眼便知端详。

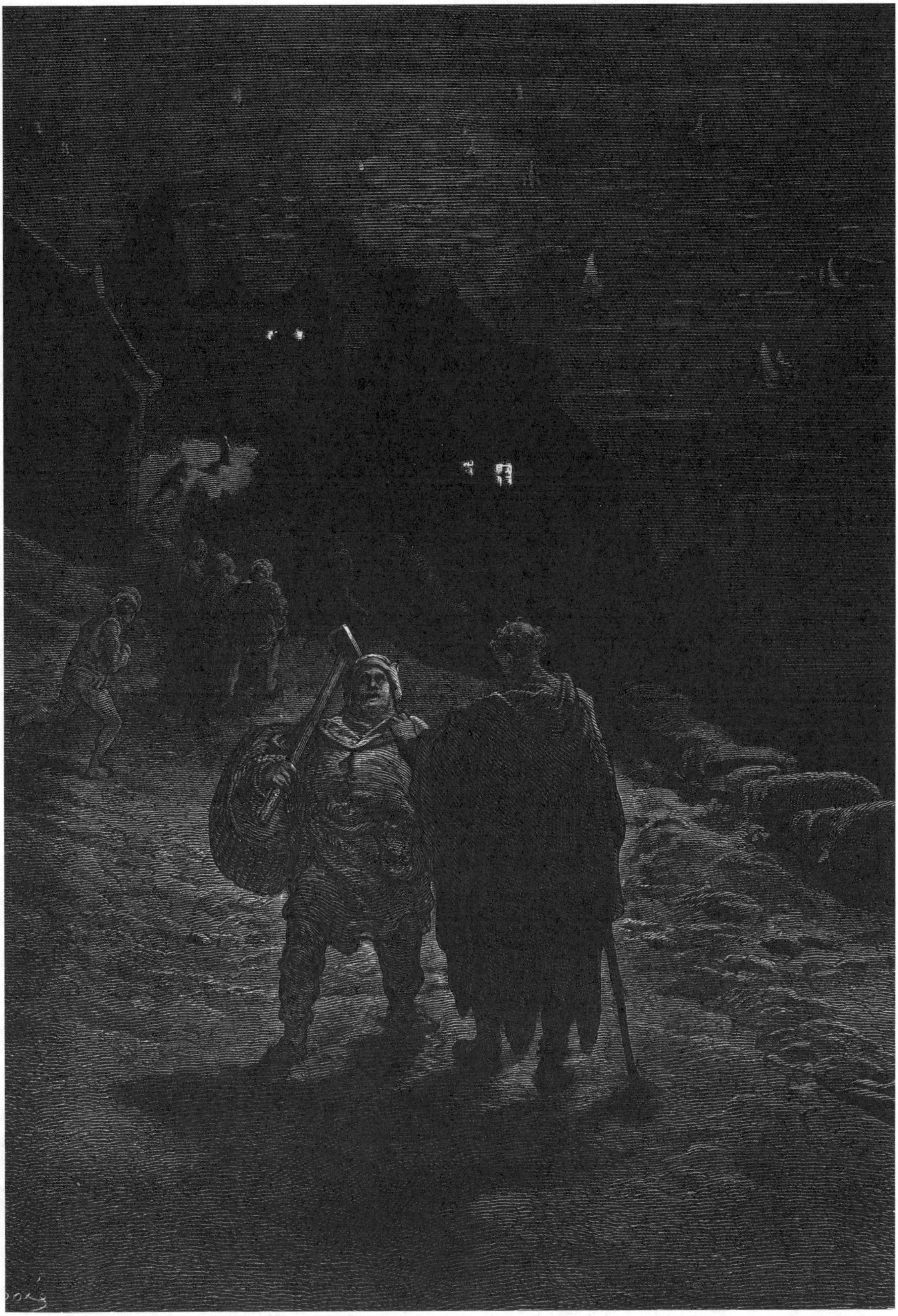

What loud uproar bursts from that door!

The wedding-guests are there:

But in the garden-bower the bride

And bride-maids singing are:

And hark the little vesper bell,

Which biddeth me to prayer!

你听那边来的喧闹！

是堂上宾客熙雍：

新妇料必歌唱园内。

但我喜晚闻祷钟！

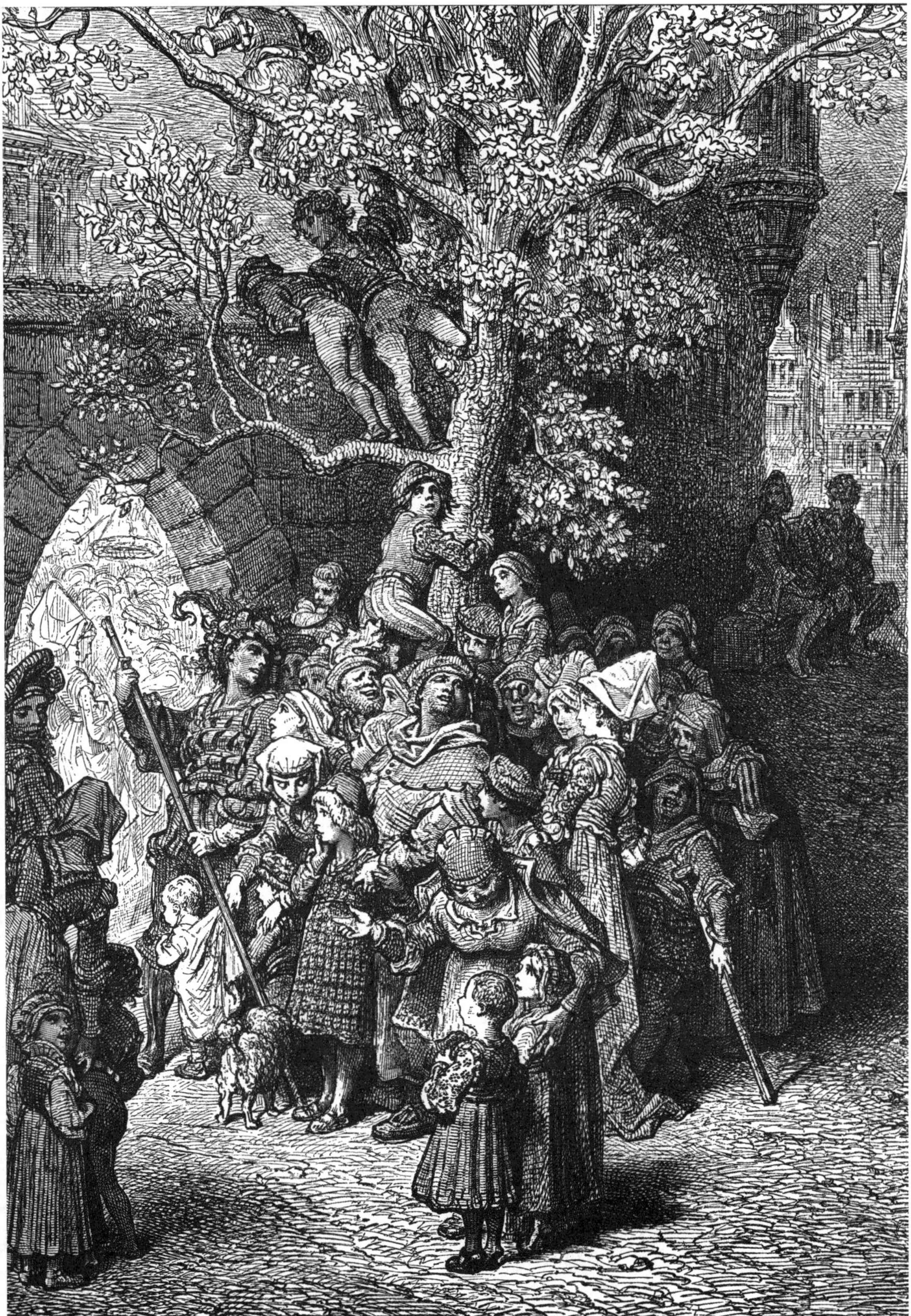

O Wedding-Guest! this soul hath been

Alone on a wide wide sea:

So lonely 'twas, that God himself

Scarce seemed there to be.

因我当时漂流大海，

四周围不见生人：

望中只有连天波浪，

船板上便是尸身。

O sweeter than the marriage-feast,

'Tis sweeter far to me,

To walk together to the kirk

With a goodly company! —

To walk together to the kirk,

And all together pray,

While each to his great Father bends,

Old men, and babes, and loving friends

And youths and maidens gay!

热闹场中非我所喜，

我只喜偕同信徒

在神座前忏悔罪孽，

让钟声净涤前污。

Farewell, farewell! but this I tell
To thee, thou Wedding-Guest!
He prayeth well, who loveth well
Both man and bird and beast.

赴宴之宾，别了，别了！
但听我临别嘱言！
爱你同类并及禽兽，
祈祷时神始垂怜。

And to teach, by his own example, love and reverence to all things that God made and loveth.
通过自己的例子，他教导他们，要热爱并尊重上帝创造的一切。

He prayeth best, who loveth best
All things both great and small;
For the dear God who loveth us,
He made and loveth all."

能爱万物，无论小大，
祈祷时神耳始倾。
因为上天造成万物，
无大小皆他宁馨。"

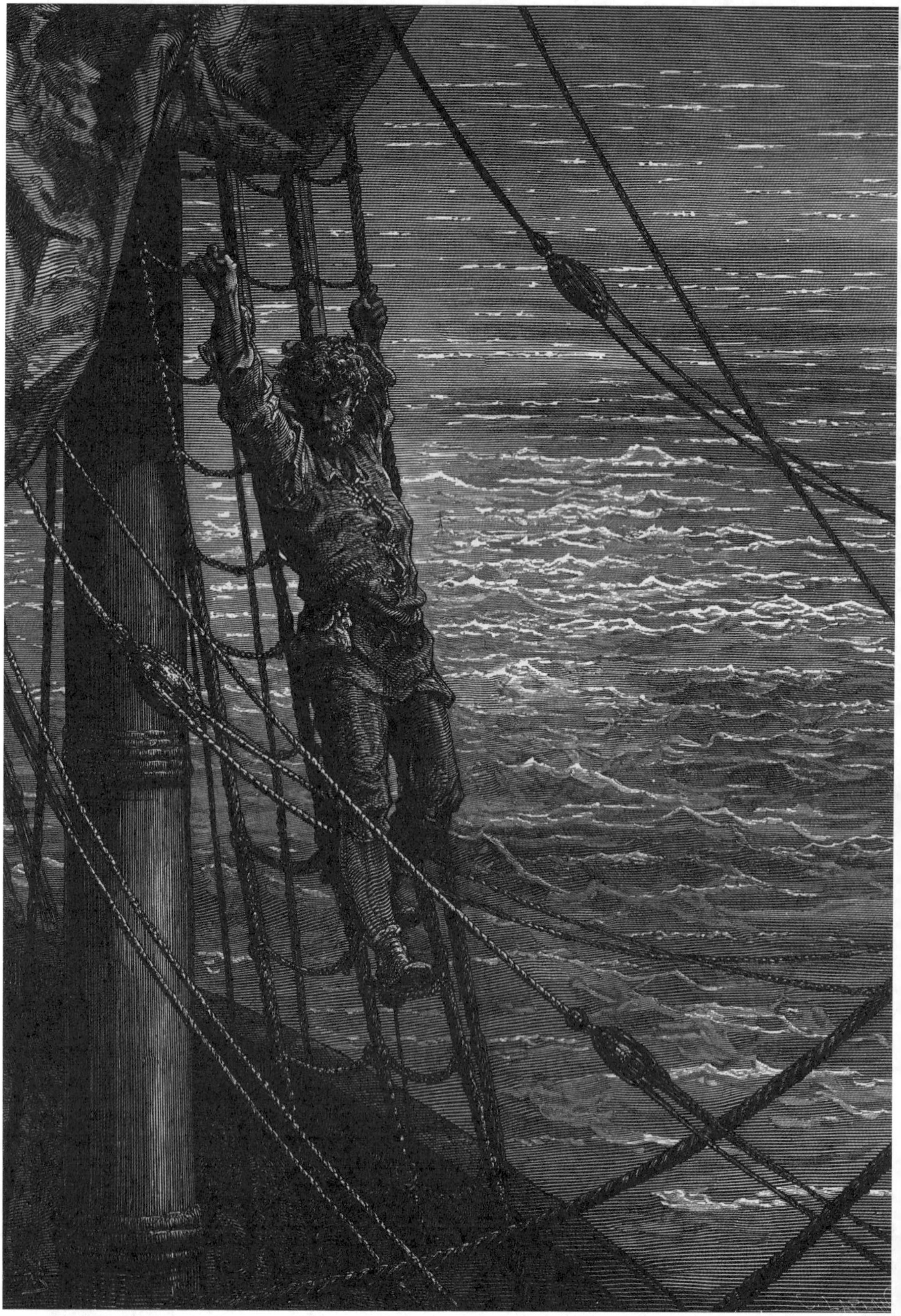

The Mariner, whose eye is bright,
Whose beard with age is hoar,
Is gone: and now the Wedding-Guest
Turned from the Bridegroom's door.

目光炯炯的那舟子，
年寿高须已斑斑，
他去了。喜宾如有失，
转声行躲避声喧。

He went like one that hath been stunned,
And is of sense forlorn:
A sadder and a wiser man,
He rose the morrow morn.

他似临头浇了冷水，
兴头已无影无踪：
他从此便识透悲乐，
将舟子常忆心中。

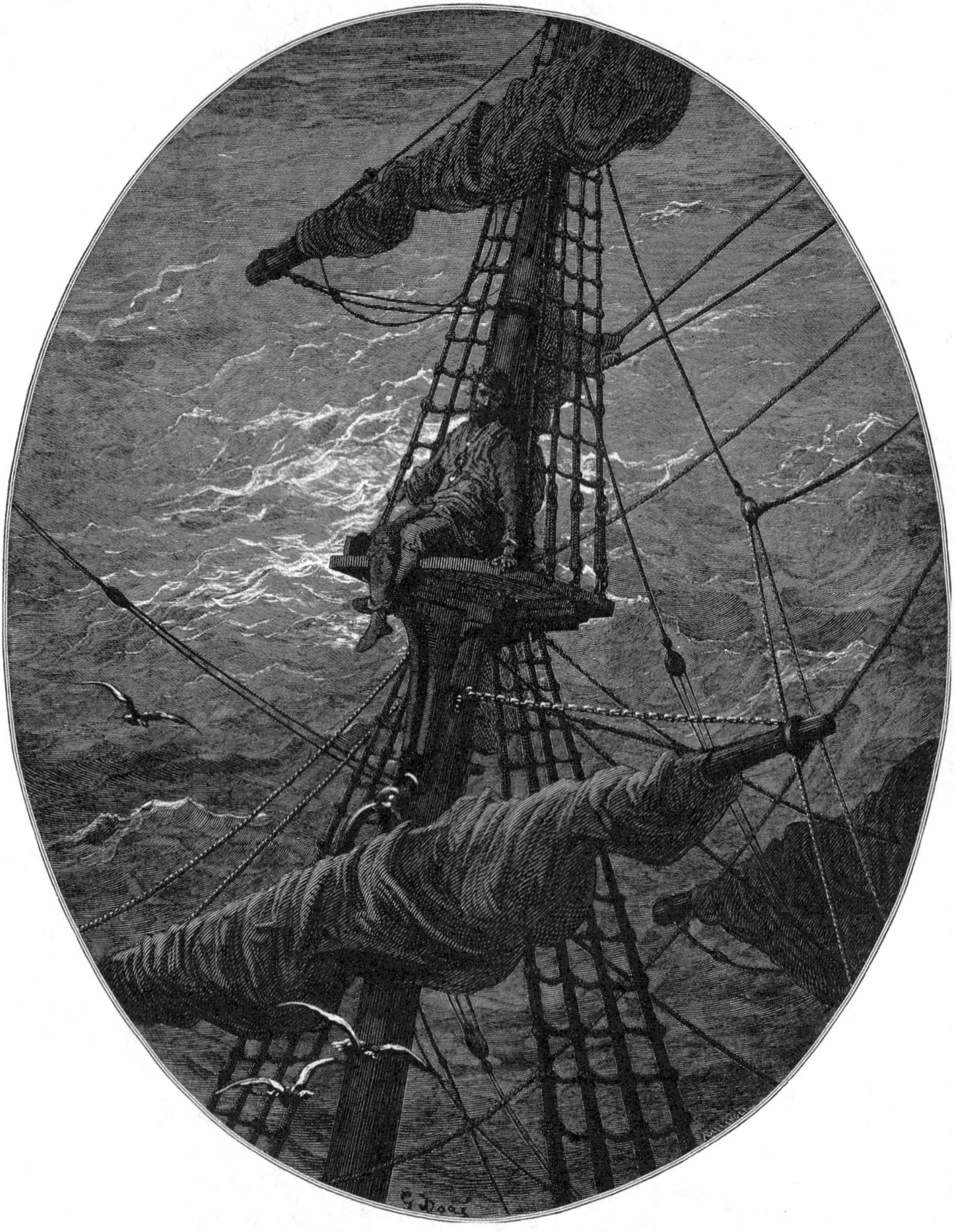
G. Doré

G Doré